The Seventh Cousin

Weekly Reader Children's Book Club *presents*

The
Seventh Cousin

by
FLORENCE LAUGHLIN

illustrated by
Sheila Greenwald

THE MACMILLAN COMPANY
NEW YORK

For
Dorothy Lessenhop
and the wonderful children
of Lincoln

Library of Congress catalog card number: 66-10163
The Macmillan Company, New York
Collier-Macmillan Canada, Ltd., Toronto, Ontario
Printed in the United States of America

This edition is published by arrangement with
The Macmillan Company

Weekly Reader Children's Book Club Edition
Senior Division

Contents

1

Apartment Number Five

"I HOPE WE find a place to live soon," said ten-year-old Patty Carter. "We've been driving around this town for ages, and I'm getting tired."

"I don't blame you, Pat," said Mr. Carter. "But you'll have to admit that we've learned a lot about Lincoln, Nebraska, in the last couple of hours. It's different from New York City, but I believe we're going to enjoy our summer here."

"Hold it, Dad!" Scott, who was twelve, suddenly shouted from the back seat. "There's a place we can look at."

His father pulled the dusty car over to the curb and put on the brakes. All four Carters looked hopefully at a sign in front of an old house.

> **TOWER ARMS**
> **APARTMENT FOR RENT**

Scott stuck his curly head out of the window and stretched his neck to look upward. "Wow!" he exclaimed. "What a mansion!"

Patty, her boredom forgotten, bumped her brother's knee in her eagerness to get to the window and see too. "It looks just like an old castle," she said. "I want to take a picture of it."

The big old-fashioned house had been a thing of glory—in its day. It had long windows of leaded glass and many gables trimmed with fancy curlicues. At one corner rose a high, rounded tower, like the guardian of some medieval palace.

There were two people in front of the house. A man on a ladder was painting the dingy gray walls a sparkling white. And a tall lanky boy was mowing the lawn.

Scott Carter just glanced at the boy at first. Then he turned back to take a second look, and his mouth fell open in amazement.

Tied to the back of the tall boy's Levi's were six or seven huge colored balloons! They bobbed in the air above him.

Patty gasped and then began to giggle. Mr. Carter looked at Mrs. Carter and shook his head from side to side. "We might be wise just to drive on and pretend we never saw this crazy place," he remarked. "What do you think, Molly?"

Mrs. Carter was already putting on the white straw hat which she kept handy in a plastic bag beside her.

"As long as we've stopped, we might as well see the

apartment," she said firmly. "It probably has anti-macassars and bathtubs with legs, but I'm like Patty—I'm tired of looking. Come, children."

As they walked toward the house the boy with the balloons turned around. He appeared to be a year or two older than Scott and had a shock of corn-colored hair above a long, serious face. He didn't seem happy at the sight of the newcomers and glanced anxiously at the Carters' travel-worn car.

"Hello." Scott's father spoke first. "We'd like to see the apartment. Where will I find the manager?"

"Manager's Mr. Hunch." The boy pointed to the man on the ladder, who was whistling a merry tune and keeping time with his paintbrush. "He's my father. I'm Elwood."

Then the boy leaned toward Mr. Carter and lowered his voice. "You won't like the apartment," he said seriously. "It's way up on the third floor—you'll have to climb a lot of steps."

Mr. Carter smiled. "We don't mind a few steps, Elwood."

"No, indeed," said his wife. "They're good for the hips."

"It's awful noisy up there, too," the boy insisted.

His balloons—red, green, and yellow—trembled above him as he spoke, and Scott could hardly contain his curiosity. What was the guy trying to prove, he wondered. He didn't dare to look at his sister for fear they'd *both* laugh.

But at the moment Patty had other ideas.

"Hold still, Elwood!" she cried unexpectedly. "I'm going to take your picture, if you don't mind." Before Elwood could say whether he minded or not, she was backing up toward the car to get a good shot of the boy and the house.

Patty Carter was a lively girl with a bright cap of hair that shone like purest gold. When she made up her mind to go after something, she usually got it.

Scott followed his father over to the man on the ladder. Mr. Hunch stopped whistling and looked down when they asked about renting the apartment.

"Yes, siree!" he said. He resembled his son Elwood, but *his* long face was more cheerful. "We have two vacancies, but number five's the one for you. Nice rooms. Beautiful view. I'll take you right up to see it."

He finished whistling his little song as he climbed down the ladder. Then the Carters followed him into the Tower Arms.

While Mr. Hunch disappeared into apartment one to get the keys, Scott eagerly looked around. They were in a large hallway, papered in gold and gray. From a door nearby came the tinkling notes of a piano and a high voice saying, "*One*, two; *one*, two—"

On that door was a tiny sign: MISS TWITTENGALE— MUSIC LESSONS.

Scott grinned to himself. Was that what Elwood meant by "noisy"?

"This must have been a fine place in the old days,"

Mr. Carter said as they all trooped up the stairway behind the manager.

"Yes, siree," Mr. Hunch agreed emphatically. "Finest house in Lincoln! Old Mrs. Truelove—she was the owner, you know—lived right here for sixty years. I was her chauffeur before she passed away. She wrote in her will that Elwood and I were to live on here and see that her wishes were carried out. So we just asked the court to let us make the house into apartments. . . . Here we are."

They had arrived in front of number five, on the third floor. The Carter family waited impatiently for Mr. Hunch to unlock the door, hardly daring to guess what they might find on the other side.

They were pleasantly surprised. The living room was large enough, with freshly painted walls and a real fireplace. Some of the furniture was antique, but the tables shone with polish.

There was a modern kitchen and bathroom and two nice bedrooms. One of them had pink rosebud wallpaper and a cushioned window seat.

"This is my room!" cried Patty when she saw it. She flew across the room and punched the mattress of the four-poster bed.

Scott began to get a little worried. He certainly didn't want pink roses, but he *did* want a place to sleep.

Mrs. Carter looked understandingly at her tall son. "You may have to sleep on the couch, dear, if we live here. Would you mind very much?"

"No, siree!" Mr. Hunch answered that. He led them briskly through the living room to a small door in the corner.

"Here's the perfect hideaway for that young man. There's a room in the tower on every floor of the house. My boy Elwood has the one below. Keeps his scientific thingamawhats in it."

Triumphantly he threw open the door, and Scott's heart gave a little leap of delight.

The tower room was almost perfectly round and about twelve feet across. There wasn't much in it—just a cot and a curve-backed chest built into one wall. But there was a wonderful row of windows around the room, revealing a limitless expanse of blue sky.

"This is the best room in the house," Scott said, perfectly satisfied. He turned expectantly to his father. "We *are* going to take the apartment, aren't we, Dad?"

"Better snap it up," advised Mr. Hunch. "Rent's only ninety a month and you won't find anything better in town. The kids will like it up here, and my son Elwood will be mighty glad to have young folks to pal with."

Scott wasn't so sure about that after the strange reception Elwood had given them. But Mr. Carter settled the matter by taking out his wallet. And Mrs. Carter sat down happily on a cherrywood love seat to make out a list of things that they would need.

Suddenly the peace was shattered.

Just as Mr. Hunch was handing Scott's father a receipt for the rent, there was a wild clatter from above. A loudly clanging bell was accompanied by a shrill demanding whine.

"What on earth was that?" cried Mrs. Carter, jumping up in alarm.

Mr. Hunch looked embarrassed.

"Oh, that's just Miss Bluebell, the heiress," he said quickly. "She lives up above. She really owns this place, you know. Old Mrs. Truelove left most of her fortune to Bluebell, and said right in her will that she was to live in this house for the rest of her life. Bluebell is a—"

Before he could say another word, the clanging noise

was repeated. This time it was joined by loud, emphatic banging.

"Oh, my! I'd better go see what she wants," Mr. Hunch said nervously. "Excuse me, folks." And he hurried out through the door.

Scott looked at Pat, and Pat looked at Scott. The girl's blue eyes were wide with curiosity. "What do you think he was going to tell us?" she asked. "Do you suppose the heiress is an old servant of the woman who owned the house?"

Scott grinned a bit weakly. "Might even be a *young* servant," he answered. "She can sure make a lot of noise." The banging was still going on.

They went to the doorway and looked down the hall —just in time to see Mr. Hunch climb a small stairway to the attic. He took out his keys and unlocked a narrow door, and as he disappeared from sight, Scott heard him say in a kindly voice: "There, there, Miss Bluebell. What's the trouble now?"

"Why, he has her locked in!" Patty whispered. "I wonder why, Scott."

"I don't know," the boy said thoughtfully. "But I'm beginning to think Dad was right when he said this was a crazy place. No wonder Elwood tried to warn us."

They had no time to ponder the mystery longer, however, for just then Mrs. Carter called them.

"I want you to go down to the car and bring up some of the luggage," she said. "We'll get our clothes put away and then go out and shop for groceries. I believe we are going to be very happy in this house."

"So do I," agreed her husband. "And it's not far from the office where I'll be working." Mr. Carter was an architect and had come to Lincoln to supervise the building of a new medical clinic. "It's such a pleasant neighborhood. At the moment, that is," he added.

He looked up at the ceiling with a puzzled frown. But the commotion from the attic had stopped, and he smiled and shrugged. The Carters weren't ones to worry too much over trifles. Especially trifles they couldn't see.

Scott and his sister raced each other down the stairs. Fortunately the steps were carpeted or they might have disturbed the peace themselves. When they reached the front door, Scott threw it open, then stopped short, blocking Patty's way.

"Do you see what I see?" he demanded. "That Elwood is snooping around our car!"

The boy was bent over the license plate, wiping it with his handkerchief. When he glanced around and saw Scott and Patty looking at him he straightened and walked quickly across the lawn. His balloons tugged at the belt of his Levi's as he disappeared around the corner of the house.

2

A Face at the Window

SCOTT WAS still pondering Elwood's strange behavior as he got ready for bed that night.

He was standing at the open windows in his room in the tower, looking out over the roofs and spires of Lincoln. The sweet summer air flowed over his face.

He could see in three directions through the curving windows. On one side he spotted the Cornhusker Hotel, where the Carters had stayed for their first night in the city after their long trip from New York. Beyond the hotel rose the gleaming dome of the capitol building, topped by the giant statue of "The Sower."

Scott breathed deeply. He liked this level land, with its gold and emerald fields and winding rivers. He liked the friendly people . . . friendly, that is, except for Elwood Hunch!

Scott frowned. What was eating that boy, he asked himself for the hundredth time. Why didn't he want the Carter family living in the old Truelove mansion?

There was something definitely odd about Elwood. And about the old house, too.

Still under the spell of its strangeness, Scott finally crawled into bed. The moonlight streamed brightly through the window. It shone on a small wrought-iron chandelier that hung above him, casting spidery shadows on the curved wall.

He dropped off to sleep, staring at the light fixture. And he awoke suddenly, in the middle of the night, still seeing it. Scott felt a creepy sensation at the back of his neck.

The chandelier was moving. Slowly it swayed, from side to side—as if swung by a ghostly hand. It made a faint creaking sound.

Earthquake! That was Scott's first thought. But when he sat up and looked around he realized that nothing else was moving. And the breeze coming through the window was too light to move a feather, let alone an iron fixture.

Silently Scott got out of bed. He had brought a chair from the living room on which to hang his clothes. He stood on it now and was just able to grab a ring that hung from the chandelier. The swaying stopped, but he could feel the tug of some unseen force pulling against him. The instant he released the ring, the eerie pendulum began to swing again.

Scott climbed down from the chair and, still in his bare feet, slipped through the living room to rouse his father.

"There's something spooky going on in my room, Dad," he whispered. "Come and see it, please."

Mr. Carter joined his son somewhat reluctantly. In the living room they met Patty in her robe and slippers.

"What's the matter?" she asked.

"Scott thinks he's cornered a ghost," Mr. Carter told her.

The chandelier was still swaying when they reached the room. The spidery shadows swung back and forth on the wall behind Scott's bed.

"What's making it swing?" asked Patty in awe.

"Strangest thing I ever saw," muttered Mr. Carter, climbing on the chair.

But the moment they spoke, the movement stopped. That was the end of it, though they waited for quite a while to see if it would begin again. Finally they went back to bed.

In the morning Scott half suspected that he had dreamed the whole silly business, but when the matter was mentioned at breakfast, he knew that he really had seen the chandelier doing a dance above his bed.

If I could just get up there in the attic, he thought, I could solve the riddle.

After breakfast Mr. Carter went downtown to his office to get started with his work. Mrs. Carter decided to rearrange the pictures on the wall, and Patty and Scott went downstairs to explore.

In the entryway by the front door was a bulletin board, and on it was a list of the tenants in the Tower Arms. Scott studied it with interest. There seemed to be just six apartments in the house, two on each floor. The Hunches and Miss Twittengale occupied the first floor, of course. The music teacher's door was ajar and they caught a glimpse of her inside—a tiny, gray-haired lady, busily dusting her piano.

On the second floor, in apartments three and four, lived someone named Caleb Jones, and a Mr. and Mrs. Penny. Mr. Hunch had already listed the new tenants in number five. Mr. and Mrs. Paul Carter. Number six was vacant.

"I wonder why he didn't list apartment seven," said Patty.

"What do you mean?" asked Scott. Then he laughed. "Oh, you mean the attic and Miss Bluebell—the heiress. I suppose everybody knows *she* lives here. After all, she owns the place."

"I sure would like to get a look at her," remarked Patty.

Outside, Mr. Hunch was already busy with his painting and whistling. He waved his brush at them. "Just make yourselves at home," he called, "Elwood's in the backyard somewhere. He'll be glad to show you around."

The property of the old Truelove place was only a couple of hundred feet wide, but it ran back through the entire block. There were several outbuildings and a small orchard with old fruit trees. Scott tasted a crab apple, but it was tiny and green and puckered his mouth. When he threw it down, a huge white goose waddled up and grabbed it.

Peeping into the old carriage house, they saw a fairly modern black sedan and a high, square electric car which looked as though it had been sitting there for half a century.

They struggled with the big doors, finally pulling them open.

Patty ran to the electric car, opened the door, and jumped inside, raising a cloud of dust as she landed on the seat. She sat there, pretending she was driving, until Scott ordered her out.

In spite of Mr. Hunch's promise, Elwood didn't come

to show them around. But Scott had the uncomfortable feeling that the boy was watching them every minute. Once he thought he saw the flash of a red balloon disappearing around the corner of the carriage house. Another time, as he and Patty came back to the rear of the old house, he was sure he saw the cellar door slam shut.

Scott was annoyed, and disappointed too. He really wanted to get to know the other boy. Patty was good company, but she was, after all, a girl. Besides, there were some questions Scott wanted to ask Elwood.

It was when they went back to the apartment for lunch that Scott and Patty chanced to meet two of the second-floor tenants. They had just started up the stairs, when they heard voices above them.

"Wait, Scott," Patty said softly, grabbing his arm. "I heard them mention 'the heiress'!" So they stood still for a moment, listening.

"She's been indisposed, poor little thing," said a woman's voice kindly. "Yesterday I took her up some of my rhubarb tea. Elwood was so pleased. He's such a nice boy and he's been so worried about her. Thinks somebody has given her something that upset her—"

"If you ask me, Mrs. Penny," came a man's voice in deep, cavernous tones, with a Boston accent, "I'd say she had too many of those green apples! I saw her in the orchard the other day stuffing herself. And, personally, I don't care," he added.

"Why, Caleb, how heartless of you! I know Miss

Bluebell is a bit mischievous at times, but she's such a cute little thing."

"Cute?" Caleb Jones sounded peevish. "Not when she makes all that racket. It gets so bad sometimes I can't concentrate on my painting. When she gets to chattering and moaning, I simply can't work."

Scott and Patty hurried on up the stairs. In the second-floor hallway they saw the speakers, who reminded Patty of Mr. and Mrs. Sprat. Caleb Jones was a tall intense young man with a proud head and longish hair. And Mrs. Penny was very short and round, with rosy cheeks and glasses.

She looked curiously at the boy and girl. Then she smiled. "You must be the new tenants in number five."

Scott nodded and paused. "Yes, ma'am. I'm Scott Carter and this is my sister, Patricia."

"Tell your mother I'll be up to call on her."

Caleb Jones held out his hand to Scott. "Glad to meet you, boy," he said. "I'm in number three. Come and see me, anytime. You can tell me what you think of my new picture. I'm going to put it in the art show— if I ever get it done."

He said the last rather sadly and Scott didn't know what to answer, so he just smiled and gave Patty a little shove. And soon they were scooting up to the third floor.

As they came in sight of the attic door, Patty paused. "I can't stand it much longer, Scott. I guess if Mrs.

Penny can take the heiress rhubarb tea, I can call on her too."

"Better not," her brother warned. "I don't think Elwood would like it."

That evening when Mr. Carter came home from work, he brought Patty's snapshots. "I've already glanced at them, Pat," he said apologetically. There was a funny look in his eyes. "I think you took a picture of the ghost in the attic."

Patty grabbed the pictures and Scott watched over her shoulder. Quickly she found the one of Elwood in front of the big house and held it up.

There was Elwood, all right, with his ridiculous balloons. There were Mr. and Mrs. Carter and Scott. And there in the highest window of the tower was something else. It looked like the figure of a small child in a light dress. The face was in shadow, but two bright eyes were plainly visible.

"Why, it's a little girl—or a doll!" cried Patty. She looked around at the rest of the family, her blue eyes questioning. "Do you suppose that could be Miss Bluebell?"

3

Meet the Heiress

IF IT HADN'T been for Miss Twittengale, Patty would never have done what she did. It happened the very next morning, when Pat and Scott left the apartment to go to the store for some milk and a box of raisins. Mrs. Carter had promised to make oatmeal cookies.

They saw the tiny, gray-haired music teacher in the hall. She was definitely coming from the attic stairway.

When she saw Scott and his sister she greeted them pleasantly. Then she said a very strange thing! "Isn't it a lovely morning? I just had to go for a walk." And she tripped on down the hall.

Scott and Patty stared after her.

"Why the sly thing!" Patty said when Miss Twittengale's head had disappeared in the stairwell. "Pretending she was out for a walk! It's perfectly clear that she has been up in the attic, calling on the heiress. And

if *she* can do it—" Patty darted toward the narrow steps
—"I guess I can!"

"Wait a minute," Scott pleaded.

But Patty had made up her mind. Before he could
stop her she was knocking on the little door. She didn't
know that Elwood had just gone inside and that the
door was unlocked. She rapped so hard that she pushed
the door open.

All of a sudden there was a screeching yelp, and out
of the door tore the heiress herself—a childlike creature
in a ruffled pink dress!

She almost knocked Patty over as she headed for the
hallway. After her came Elwood, shouting at the top of
his lungs.

"Now see what you've done! Miss Bluebell, Miss
Bluebell, come back here!"

But Miss Bluebell had tasted freedom and she
wasn't going to give it up so easily. She glanced around
wildly, and spotting Scott, she landed with a bound on
his shoulder. Before the boy could blink twice, she was
off again.

She leaped from Scott to a red fire extinguisher on
the wall. For a moment she sat there, her teeth showing in a wide, toothy grin. She seemed to be teasing
Elwood, daring him to catch her.

Patty now stood beside her brother, and they both
stared in stunned silence at the amazing little creature. Miss Bluebell, the heiress to the Truelove mansion, was a monkey! A small, hairy brown animal in a

child's pink pinafore with a jaunty blue ribbon on her tail.

Scott looked curiously from the monkey to Elwood. For the first time he noticed the boy wasn't wearing his balloons. But he *was* wearing his most woeful expression.

"You shouldn't have let her out," he said accusingly to Patty. "She's always hard to catch when she's been cooped up for a while."

"I'm sorry," mumbled Patty. "But I never dreamed she was a monkey."

"Be a good girl, Miss Bluebell." Elwood started to

walk cautiously toward the fire extinguisher, holding out his arms. "Let's go back and finish our cornmeal mush."

Bluebell wasn't to be tempted by cornmeal mush. Just as Elwood reached her she skittered away, this time in the direction of the main stairs. Landing on the banisters, she went sliding and skipping down to the second floor.

Elwood bolted after her, followed closely by the excited Scott and Patty.

Bluebell waited mischievously on the second-floor landing until the anxious Elwood was only inches from her. Then with a saucy wave of her hand, she was off again down the hall!

Unfortunately Caleb Jones had just left his apartment to empty his trash basket, foolishly leaving his door open. Miss Bluebell vanished through it.

By the time her pursuers caught up with her, she had bounded through the artist's untidy living room and was in his studio in the tower. Perched on a tall stool in front of an easel, she was busily wielding a paintbrush!

Caleb Jones was an abstract painter, and the huge canvas in front of Miss Bluebell was very abstract indeed. From Scott's point of view, it didn't look like anything much at all. It was just a great mass of yellow blobs and black scribbles.

But it was Mr. Jones's masterpiece, and Miss Bluebell was trying to improve it. She had grabbed a brush full of red paint from a nearby table and was joyously smearing the canvas with bright crimson streaks.

Elwood emitted a moan of pure anguish, and turned to Scott. "Close the door," he ordered. "We can catch her now that we've got her penned in."

Scott obeyed, and Elwood moved toward the busy Bluebell. She sensed his approach and glanced around. With a shrill squeal, she dropped the brush and leaped right into Patty's arms!

Patty gasped, then began to laugh. "She likes me!" She hugged the small, wiry body. In response, Miss Bluebell put her hands in Patty's short, golden hair, mussing it up and chattering with pleasure.

Elwood was so relieved to have the monkey captured he actually forgot to be angry. "She likes your pretty hair," he said. "She loves anything that shines. Come now, Bluebell." He held out his arms to the monkey. "Let's go back home."

But Bluebell would have nothing to do with him. She put her arms around Patty and gave her a big sloppy kiss on the cheek.

Patty was flattered by this show of affection. "She's a darling," she said. "I'll carry her for you. Is she really the owner of this house?"

Elwood nodded and his anxious expression returned. "Yes, she is," he answered. "In fact, she inherited most of the Truelove fortune."

Scott couldn't keep from laughing. "I never heard of anything so crazy," he said. "Leaving a fortune to a monkey!"

"Old Mrs. Truelove was pretty fond of Miss Blue-bell," Elwood said defensively. "Besides, she isn't just an ordinary monkey. She has a high I.Q. That means she's very intelligent."

"Didn't Mrs. Truelove have any relatives to leave her money to?"

"She just had one son, and he died before she did, but there are some distant cousins—"

Elwood broke off suddenly. "We'd better get out of here." He took a last despairing look at the weird painting on the easel. "Mr. Jones is going to be plenty mad," he added.

Patty carried Miss Bluebell into the hall, followed by the two boys. They got out in the nick of time. When they were only a few steps from his door, Caleb Jones appeared at the head of the back stairway carrying his empty trash basket.

"Hold on there, Elwood," he called. "I want to talk to you."

The trio waited reluctantly. The artist glared at Miss Bluebell and the monkey glared right back.

"I see the heiress has recovered from her illness," he said sarcastically.

Elwood nodded.

"Too bad. If you don't keep her under better control, I'm going to have to move from Tower Arms. Just having her under the same roof upsets me dreadfully."

"Yes, sir!" Poor Elwood backed away nervously. But Caleb Jones wasn't through yet.

"I'm working on the greatest painting of my entire career, Elwood," he declared. "Six months I've spent on it, and I must have peace and quiet in order to finish it in time for the art show. Only last night," he went on, with a dramatic gesture of his hand, "I got up in the middle of the night and added a few perfect strokes by moonlight. . . . Why, I forgot to examine it this morning! I must go and see how it looks."

He dashed through his door, and the four culprits escaped to the third floor.

"Oh, brother!" breathed Scott. "Wait till he sees what Miss Bluebell did to his masterpiece."

When they reached the attic door, the little monkey still resisted Elwood's efforts to take her, so Patty had to carry her inside.

Scott didn't mind at all. He had been as eager as his sister to see the inside of "apartment seven."

4

Miss Bluebell's Abode

WHEN SCOTT CARTER entered the attic behind Elwood and Patty, he felt as though he had blundered into midgetland. He stood gazing like a startled giant.

The entire attic had been turned into an apartment for Miss Bluebell, and everything in it had been scaled down to her small size. There was a tiny couch and chair upholstered in green plastic, and small flowered rugs were scattered over the floor. On a child-sized dining table stood a half-empty glass of milk and a small bowl of mush.

The first thing Miss Bluebell did when Patty let her down was to hop to her rocking chair. She picked up a Teddy bear and sat down, rocking and cooing as she cuddled the toy in her arms.

Patty shook her blond head in disbelief, then burst into delighted laughter. "It's wonderful, Elwood," she declared. "I feel like Snow White when she visited the dwarfs!"

Then Patty had to run around and touch everything, open the miniature cabinets and peep into dresser drawers. In the clothes closet under the eaves were a whole row of dresses, fancy straw hats, and even strange little shoes.

At sight of her pretty clothes, Bluebell suddenly dropped the toy bear and went to Patty. She danced about, pointing to the closet and whining.

"She loves to dress up," said Elwood. "She's very vain."

To Scott's surprise, the boy's long face was actually glowing. It was clear that he was proud to show off his small charge and her unusual apartment. For the moment he seemed to have forgotten his distrust of the newcomers from the East.

Patty looked down at the little monkey. "Then why do you let her wear that dirty pink pinafore?" she demanded crossly. "I'm sure it hasn't been washed lately."

Elwood looked uncomfortable. "It's the only thing I can get on her without a lot of trouble," he admitted. "She's awful wiggly."

Of course Patty decided that she must change Bluebell's clothes. She looked through the closet and picked out a red-and-white playsuit. She changed the blue ribbon for a red one and even put a pair of the funny little shoes on the monkey's hind paws. They were very like soft leather moccasins.

While Patty was busy playing house with this fascinating live doll, Elwood showed Scott the rest of the

attic apartment. There was a real bathroom with a tiny
tub and shower, and a bedroom with toy-sized furniture. Scott had to stoop to go through the doors.

Then in the corner of the attic he spotted the door
which he knew must lead to the tower room above his
own. "What's in there?" he asked eagerly.

"That's Bluebell's playroom. We keep her in there
when she's not with us so she won't get mischievous
and wreck things. Come on, I'll show you."

The first thing Scott noticed was that the windows
of the tower room, like those in the rest of the attic,
were screened inside with heavy wire. He looked curiously at the floor. Except for a big rubber ball and a
child's tricycle, it was bare and smooth, and exactly
like that in his own room just below.

There seemed to be no way for anybody to reach

through and move the light fixture on the third-floor ceiling. He was no nearer to solving *that* ghostly business than he had been before.

Scott thought of telling Elwood about the strange experience, but it seemed so foolish at the moment, that he decided to wait.

He looked up at the ceiling. As this was the top room of the tower, it was shaped like an upside-down cone. From it hung Bluebell's swings and exercise bars. There was also a brass bell with a rope pull.

"Bluebell rings that when she wants attention," Elwood explained.

"I know." Scott grinned. "We heard it yesterday. She sure made a racket. We figured that the heiress to the Truelove fortune must be a pretty crazy character."

Elwood looked intently at Scott. "Do you mean that you really didn't know about Miss Bluebell *before* you came here?" he asked.

"Of course not," declared Scott. "How could we? We just got into town this week."

"There are ways," said Elwood darkly. "Plenty of people know about Mrs. Truelove's will, and some of them would like to get control of this property. The minute I laid eyes on your father, I thought he looked like one of the seven cousins."

"What seven cousins?" Scott asked anxiously.

But Elwood apparently figured he had said enough.

He turned and stalked quickly out of the tower room.

Scott was at his heels. "You're going to have to explain that, Elwood," he said, getting in front of the other boy. "My dad has never been to Nebraska before in his life. We're from New York—"

"That's just it," said Elwood stubbornly. "Some of the other heirs live on Long Island, in New York—and some in Boston."

"Is that why you didn't want us to rent an apartment here?" Scott demanded. "Because we're from New York, and because my father looks like somebody's cousin?"

Elwood nodded. "We have enough trouble right now —Bluebell and I do," he said glumly. "There's already somebody under this roof who's trying to kidnap the heiress."

"Kidnap?" Patty looked up in astonishment. She was now sitting beside the monkey at the tiny dining table. Bluebell had a bib around her neck and was obediently finishing her mush. "But why?"

Elwood Hunch sighed deeply. "Well, as long as you know this much, I might as well tell you all about it." He walked over to the small couch and sat down. He looked very odd, with his knees drawn up almost to his chin.

Scott parked himself on a miniature piano bench. "You said old Mrs. Truelove didn't have any close relatives to leave her fortune to," he said.

"That's right. Pa told me she had a son once who lived in California. But he and his wife and kid were drowned a long time ago."

"Oh, how dreadful!" said Patty. "How did it happen?"

"They had a private boat and went for a cruise in the ocean and they never came back. Pieces of the boat were found, so people figured it was wrecked in a storm."

"Poor Mrs. Truelove. She must have been very lonely all by herself in this big house."

"Maybe so," said Elwood. "Of course, she had my folks here, and me, after I was born. My mother was Mrs. Truelove's housekeeper. We lived in the rooms over the carriage house, and Pa and I just stayed on, after Ma died. . . . Then there were the pets," he added. "Mrs. Truelove sure liked animals."

"She must have," put in Scott, looking about him with renewed wonder. "I still can't get over the idea of a little monkey inheriting a house, with her own apartment. It looks almost new."

"The furniture is. Mrs. Truelove had everything made to order for Bluebell, and she let me help plan it," Elwood said proudly. "Bluebell is going to stay right here as long as she lives, and I'm supposed to stay and take care of her. That's what the will says."

"Then what happens?" asked Patty.

"Then what's left of the fortune goes to Mrs. Truelove's heirs."

"Those seven cousins, I suppose," said Scott.

"Yes, if no closer relative turns up, those cousins will get everything. They all live in the East, and they are pretty angry about Bluebell being the heiress. They even sent a lawyer out to try to break the will. And for all I know," he went on, "one of them may be living under this very roof—and up to no good."

"Don't you know the names of these cousins?" asked Scott.

"Yes. But anyone can use a fake name. If Bluebell disappeared and couldn't be found, they'd get the money—don't you see?"

Scott nodded. The idea of kidnaping a monkey still seemed a little foolish to him.

"Besides—" Elwood looked around as though he feared somebody might be listening, then lowered his voice—*"I've got evidence.* And Bluebell helped me get it."

Scott made the mistake of laughing. "Now she's a detective as well as an heiress!"

Elwood got huffy at that. "You shouldn't laugh. Bluebell is smarter than you think. I've taught her all kinds of tricks. She can ride her trike and wash her own face. I've even been teaching her to talk—"

"No!" cried Patty.

Elwood flushed. "Chimpanzees can say some words. Of course Bluebell isn't a chimp, but she's just as smart. We haven't progressed very far, but—"

All of a sudden Bluebell herself joined the conversa-

tion. With one hand she pounded on her table, with the other she held out her small plastic bowl, which was now empty. At the same time she opened her mouth and said a word.

"*Mruyrp!*" she yelped. At least that is what it sounded like to Scott. But Elwood jumped to his feet with a shout of joy.

"There! Didn't I tell you?" he cried. "Bluebell said 'more' just as plain as anything!"

"*Mruyrp,*" Bluebell said again.

Elwood turned to her. "You can't have any more just now," he explained, as though she were an intelligent child. "We used all the cornmeal and we can't make more mush till we go to the store."

"The store!" Patty suddenly clapped her hand over her mouth. "Oh, Scott, we forgot to get the milk and raisins Mother sent us after."

"You're right," said her brother, on his feet now. "We'd better get going." He turned to Elwood. "Mother's going to make us some oatmeal cookies today," he told him. "Why don't you and Bluebell come to number five this afternoon and help us eat them? Mother is just as anxious as we were to meet the heiress."

Elwood didn't hesitate long. He rewarded Scott with a shy smile. "We'd sure like that, wouldn't we, Bluebell?"

Bluebell promptly turned her empty bowl upside down on her head and grinned her acceptance of the invitation.

After Scott and Patty had left the attic, Scott turned to his sister.

"Have we been dreaming, Pat?" he asked. "Did we really meet a monkey who sits in a rocking chair and has her own private bathtub?"

5

Company for Tea

SCOTT AND PATTY wasted no time after that in getting
to the store to buy the milk and raisins. When they returned, they almost bumped into somebody who was
backing out of the door of the Tower Arms. It was the
artist, Caleb Jones, trying to maneuver his huge canvas through the door.

He was very excited, and when he saw Scott and
Patty he insisted that they take time right then to view
his masterpiece. He set it up on the lawn in front of a
tree and backed away to stand beside Scott.

"Isn't it exquisite?" he cried. "I've always felt that I
had a touch of genius, now I'm sure of it. Isn't it beautiful, boy?" he demanded of Scott.

In his confusion Scott almost said, "Yes, siree!" But
he caught himself in time and just gulped.

The awful truth was that the picture was exactly
as he had last seen it—after Bluebell had added her
"monkeyshines" with the red paint. Poor Jones thought

he had done it himself when he got up in the middle of the night and painted by moonlight.

Scott wanted to warn Patty not to tattle on Bluebell. But it wasn't necessary, for Patty was too kindhearted to disillusion the man. "Where are you taking it?" she asked.

"To Pershing Center—that big auditorium over near the capitol building." Mr. Jones walked over and boosted the canvas onto his shoulder. "I'm entering it in the show," he added. "The Arts and Crafts Society and the Gem and Mineral Club are having a combined exhibition, beginning next Friday. I want you both to promise to come."

He seemed so earnest about it that Scott agreed readily. "We'll be there," he said.

They stood on the porch, watching the artist go proudly toward town, the huge picture rising like a sail above him.

"Do you suppose he really thinks he's a good artist?" Patty asked in a puzzled tone.

"I don't know," answered her brother. "I sort of like the picture the way Bluebell finished it. But he could be just putting on an act. Remember what Elwood said about the other heirs to Mrs. Truelove's property who would like to break the will."

"He might be one of the seven cousins," said Patty.

Scott didn't want to suspect the artist. He rather liked Caleb, yet he couldn't help wondering. A moment later, when he passed Miss Twittengale's door on his way upstairs, he began to wonder about her, too.

He remembered seeing her on the third floor the day before. What had she really been doing up there near Bluebell's attic door?

By the time Scott and Patty arrived at number five, Mrs. Carter was getting a bit impatient. It was so near lunchtime, in fact, that she was about to abandon the cooky-making project. But when Patty told her they had met Elwood and had invited him and a friend for refreshments, she gave in. They decided to keep the identity of "the friend" a secret, as a surprise.

"If I make the cookies," she agreed, taking the paper sack from Scott, "you two will have to get busy too. Patty, you can cut that fresh paper for the pantry shelves while Scott takes our empty suitcases down to the basement storeroom."

She turned to her son. "I've already arranged for Mr. Hunch to meet you down there."

Scott had to make two trips with the luggage. The cellar under the old house was an eerie place, full of discarded knickknacks and old furniture. Cobwebs gleamed in the light of a small bare bulb that hung from the ceiling.

"Got to get this place cleaned up one of these days," said Mr. Hunch, helping the boy lift the cases to a shelf. "All Mrs. Truelove's personal stuff is stored down here and we can't get rid of it, of course, till the estate is finally settled."

He looked at Scott with a twinkle in his eye. "Elwood just told me you met the heiress herself this morning. What do you think of our Miss Bluebell?"

"She's quite a character," Scott answered enthusiastically. "Elwood really has her well trained."

"Yep, Elwood's a smart boy—wants to be a scientist when he grows up." His long face suddenly grew serious. "You know, Scott, I'm real glad you came to Tower Arms," he said. "Elwood needs a normal boy like you to talk to. He's a good boy, but he *thinks* too much."

"What do you mean, Mr. Hunch?"

"Well, he's always imagining things. Why, you know, he thinks there's someone in this house who wants to do away with Bluebell." The man laughed at the very idea. "Might be a little odd—some of the folks living here," he admitted, "but there isn't a one of 'em would harm a hair of that little monkey's head!"

Scott didn't know what to think. He frowned as he left the cellar, but when he opened his own door minutes later, he forgot the matter entirely. The warm spicy smell of baking cookies met him and he could hardly wait to sink his teeth into one.

At four o'clock Elwood and Bluebell appeared at the door of the apartment. Scott called his mother from the kitchen.

When Mrs. Carter walked in and saw the pert little monkey standing in the middle of the living room, she was speechless. And when Miss Bluebell was introduced to her as the heiress, and walked up and solemnly held out a paw to shake hands, Mrs. Carter had to sit down to recover her poise.

On the whole, Miss Bluebell behaved in a very lady-like manner at the little party. She sat on a kitchen stool, drank milk from a cup, and devoured as many of the delicious cookies as the watchful Elwood would allow.

Afterward she graciously entertained the group with her tricks. She turned handsprings expertly, and danced

a little jig while Elwood solemnly sang and clapped for her.

As for Elwood, he seemed to have lost his suspicions of the Carter family and thoroughly enjoyed himself. When it was time to leave, he shook hands with Scott's mother and thanked her. And Bluebell leaned over and gave Mrs. Carter one of her affectionate smacks.

At the door Elwood paused. "I'd better ask you before we go if you're missing anything. Bluebell can't help it, but she's a kleptomaniac."

"Kleptomaniac?" echoed Patty.

"That means she takes things that don't belong to her. I'd better check."

He felt in the pockets of Bluebell's playsuit. In one

he discovered a cooky which he considerately put back. From another he drew a small penknife which Scott recognized as belonging to him.

"Why, the little pickpocket," he said with a laugh. "When did she swipe that?"

Elwood held up something else. It was one of the shiny objects that Bluebell found irresistible, a small golden comb.

Mrs. Carter gasped. "You rascal!" she said to Bluebell. And as she took the comb and put it back into the thick coil of hair at the back of her head, the small monkey hid her face with her hands.

When Bluebell moved one finger and a bright brown eye peeped out, they all laughed. "You're forgiven," said Mrs. Carter.

Soon after the guests had departed, Mr. Carter returned from his office. He seemed a little shaken.

"Did I see what I *think* I did?" he demanded, looking around at the faces of his family. "I just met Elwood on the stairs, and unless I'm wrong, he had a monkey in his arms. A monkey dressed in a girl's clothes —eating a cooky!"

"You saw it, Dad," Scott admitted with a grin. "And wait till you hear who that monkey is. She's none other than the owner of the Tower Arms apartments—the heiress herself."

"And," added Mrs. Carter, "that monkey just left this apartment. She joined us at tea."

"Give me strength," sighed Mr. Carter. He took off

his hat and collapsed in a big leather chair. "Never thought I'd live to see the day when I'd have a member of the ape family for a landlady."

Mrs. Carter brought her husband a cup of tea and a plate of cookies. While he revived himself, Patty and Scott sat on the couch and related their recent adventures. They told him all about Miss Bluebell and her enchanting living quarters in the attic, and about Mrs. Truelove's peculiar will and the mysterious seven cousins who wanted to break it.

"And the reason Elwood didn't want us around here," said Scott with a laugh, "was because he thought *you* looked like one of those cousins, Dad."

"I may look like one of them, Scott, but I'm certainly not one of the heirs. I'm afraid we don't have any rich relatives."

"It is a strange case, though, Paul," Mrs. Carter remarked. "I never heard of anything so eccentric—leaving a fortune to a monkey!"

"It's unusual, all right," said Mr. Carter, "but not unprecedented. Wealthy people have often willed large sums of money for the support of a beloved pet—usually a cat or dog. And I've read about a parrot in possession of a huge house such as this, in Canada. As long as the parrot lives the house can't be torn down."

"Parrots sometimes live a long time," put in Scott with a laugh. "You remember Captain Flint in *Treasure Island*, Patty? Long John said he might even be two hundred years old!"

"No wonder the seven cousins are impatient," said Patty. "Miss Bluebell might outlive them all."

"By the way," Mr. Carter asked, "you didn't chance to meet that ghost in the attic, did you, son? The one that moves chandeliers with invisible hands."

"No," admitted Scott. "But somehow I think that Elwood had a hand in that business. The more I see him, the more complicated I think he is."

"Complicated or crazy, Scott," said Patty, jumping suddenly to her feet. "We got so interested in Bluebell and her tricks we even forgot to ask him why he was wearing those balloons yesterday!"

"We sure did." Scott Carter scratched his dark, curly head. "There are a lot of questions I mean to have answered before we leave the Tower Arms."

6

Defying Gravity

SCOTT FULLY intended to keep a watchful eye on the mysterious chandelier when he went to bed that night. But it had been a busy day and he was fast asleep almost as soon as he shut off the light.

He was awakened in the morning by the impatient clanging of Bluebell's gong from the room above. Moments later he heard Elwood's drawling voice. He got out of bed and quickly put on his clothes. When he looked out into the hall he saw Elwood and Bluebell just coming down from the attic. Bluebell was wearing a harness today and the tall boy was leading her with a light chain.

"Morning," he said, when he saw Scott's curly head sticking out of the door. "Bluebell and I are going to do some experiments. Want to come along?"

"Sure," said Scott eagerly.

"Can I come, too?" Patty stuck her blond head over

her brother's shoulder. At the sight of her the little monkey jumped up and down and clapped.

Elwood's long face lit up slightly with his shy smile. "Looks like Bluebell wants you to," he said.

"I'll go tell Mother and get my sweater."

The two boys sauntered off and Patty caught up with them in the lower hall.

"We have to go to my place first and get the balloons," Elwood said, opening the door of number one. "Pa's up already and outside, painting."

Inside the first-floor tower room, Scott could only gaze in wonder. The place had been converted into a perfect little laboratory.

Below the windows had been built a row of curved cabinets. There was a sink with running water, a Bunsen burner, a great variety of flasks and tubes, and endless jars and boxes of chemicals. On a shelf was a row of weighty books, with names on the covers like Einstein and Kepler.

And there were Elwood's balloons! Weirdly, like something in a dream, they clung to the ceiling in a colorful cloud—strings hanging down.

"Is this all yours?" Scott asked in awe.

"Yep," the other boy said modestly. "I'm going to be a scientist—maybe a nuclear physicist. Right now, I'm experimenting with gravitational force."

It was about that moment that Scott spied a big electromagnet under a wooden cabinet. Several small iron objects were stuck to it. "Where'd you get that?" he asked, pointing.

"I ordered it through an ad in *Science News Letter*," the boy answered. "I've done a lot of work with it."

A slow grin grew over Scott's face. "You didn't by any chance do some experimenting with it up in the attic the other night, did you?"

Elwood looked sheepish. "Guess I did," he admitted. "I figured if you thought the house was haunted, you might go away. There's a loose board in the floor up there. By holding that heavy magnet just above the light fixture in your room, and moving it from side to side, I created a powerful pull on the chain and—"

Patty broke in, laughing. "You were wasting your time, Elwood. It takes a lot more than a ghost in the attic to scare the Carter family."

Scott silently agreed. But he was glad to have the "ghost" explained, just the same. And now it looked as though they were close to solving the mystery of the balloons.

Elwood had begun to pull them down, one by one. He handed some to Scott and some to Patty. "These are filled with helium, which is lighter than air, as you know," he explained. "I have a theory that with the help of these balloons I can make people's work easier."

"Is that what you were trying to do when you mowed the lawn the other day?" asked Patty.

Elwood frowned. "Well, that experiment was a failure. I found that the balloons sort of pulled me backward and made it even harder to push the mower."

Scott gazed at his new friend with profound respect.

"Today," Elwood went on, "we will test the efficiency of lighter-than-air balloons in mountain climbing. They should make the body feel lighter and make climbing easier."

"But where are we going to find a mountain?" asked Scott. "I haven't even seen a good-sized hill around here."

"Well, we have to make do with what we have." Elwood was by now backing out of the room, carefully guarding his balloons. Scott and Patty followed.

"We haven't had breakfast," said Patty. "Wait here." Scott held her balloons while she ran upstairs to grab some apples and cookies for them to munch on.

Soon they were parading down the sidewalks of Lincoln—Elwood in the lead, with Bluebell hopping along at the rear on her leash. Scott felt a bit silly, being tugged along by his bunch of balloons whenever a puff of wind caught them. But he had to admit they did make him feel lighter. He fairly bounced.

The "mountain" proved to be the wide flight of steps in front of the capitol building—right in the heart of town.

"You go first, Scott," Elwood suggested, "and I'll observe you." He carefully calculated the number of balloons necessary for the younger boy's weight and added a few of his own.

Wrapping the strings securely around his hand, Scott went soaring up the steps, turned around, and came floating down again.

A crowd of people soon gathered, bewildered by the amazing spectacle, but Scott was not the least self-conscious now. The antigravity device made him light-headed as well as light of foot, and he had a glorious time. All in the interest of science!

Patty had a few turns, with a smaller number of bal-

loons. Then Elwood himself took over. He was deadly serious about the whole business. He stopped every now and then to check his pulse and make notes in his record book.

Bystanders didn't know what to think about the awkward, yellow-haired boy who went bounding gravely up and down the steps. The experiment caused quite a few people to be late for work and generally upset the business of the capitol that day. The governor missed his morning root-beer break; and a little blue-eyed librarian who worked in the building declared that something should be done about these "juvenile delinquents."

Bluebell was the only one left out of the game. She tugged at Elwood's pants legs and pleaded pitifully for a turn, but he refused.

"She might sail off and we'd never catch her," he said. So she sulked behind Patty's legs until Elwood decided it was time to go home.

When the young people arrived back at the Tower Arms they found plump Mrs. Penny, in a lavender dress, sitting in a rocking chair on the porch. She was talking to Caleb, who sat on the steps, and when she saw the pouting Bluebell, she called her over and petted her.

"The dear little thing," she said. Then she reached into her pocket and got a peanut for her.

Mrs. Penny and the artist didn't seem the least bit

curious about the balloons. Scott decided that the tenants in the Tower Arms were used to Elwood's strange antics. Caleb Jones didn't even speak to Elwood and he glared with distaste at poor Bluebell.

"He doesn't like her," Elwood said moodily when they were once more back in his laboratory. They released the balloons and let them fly up to the ceiling. "I'm suspicious of Caleb Jones. I think he's the one who broke into Bluebell's apartment last month."

"What makes you think that?" Scott asked. "You said you had evidence, but you didn't tell us what it was."

Elwood reached into his pocket. "Look at this," he said, holding out his hand. On his palm was a round leather button with a spiral design on top. "Bluebell tore this from the clothes of whoever it was tried to kidnap her. And I wouldn't be surprised if Caleb Jones has a coat in his closet with this very button missing."

"Tell us what happened, Elwood," Patty insisted, breathless with excitement.

But before the boy could continue Mrs. Carter's voice was heard in the hallway.

"Scott, Patty," she called. "Where are you? Come upstairs and have your breakfast."

Patty sighed. "Maybe we can see you again after we eat," she said hopefully.

"Yes," put in Scott. "If there really is something

funny going on around here, we might be able to help you get to the bottom of it."

"Three heads are better than one," said Elwood. He took Bluebell's leash from Patty. "The heiress and I will be up in her apartment. Come up there, if you can, as soon as you're finished. I'll tell you all I know."

7

Three Detectives

IT WAS mid-afternoon before the three young people finally met again in the attic to discuss the mystery. Mr. Hunch had decided that Elwood had done enough scientific experimenting for one day and had set him to weeding the flower beds. And Mrs. Carter, who had the annoying belief that "busy hands make better brains," had kept her two children occupied doing errands.

By now Patty and Scott were almost bursting with suspense. "What makes you so sure somebody wants to kidnap Bluebell?" the girl asked. They all sat on the floor around the low table. The little monkey was closed in the tower room.

"Well, it's this way—" Elwood paused to reach for some peanuts Patty had brought along. "It was on a Saturday and Pa and I were going to Omaha to my cousin's wedding. We forgot the present and had to come back to get it, *and*—" he waited dramatically for a few seconds—"when we drove up in front, I saw somebody through the window of the tower."

"Was the attic locked?"

"Not then. We never thought anybody would want to harm poor little Bluebell. I ran up the stairs as fast as I could, but whoever it was must have seen us through the window and had scooted off. But the door was open, a chair was knocked over—and Bluebell was all scared and fussed up when I got to her."

"That's when you found the leather button," Scott prompted.

"Yep. Pa didn't think anybody broke in. He thinks she just picked the button up somewhere else and kept it in her pocket, like she does other things."

"Why do you feel so sure Caleb is guilty? I know he doesn't like Bluebell, but lots of people can't stand monkeys."

"I know," admitted Elwood, "but Caleb Jones talks with that Boston accent, and anyway, I just have a *feeling*. I think he's one of those cousins and can't wait to get his share of Bluebell's fortune."

"It could be one of the other tenants," put in Patty. "Miss Twittengale, for instance." She told about meeting the music teacher in the third-floor hall, where she certainly didn't belong.

"I saw her there, too," said Elwood. "She told me she was out for a walk."

Patty laughed. "Seems mighty silly to me, taking a walk in old dark halls when you could be out in the

sunshine. Then there are those Pennys—I think I saw
Mr. Penny in the hall yesterday—"

"Oh, no, you couldn't have," said Elwood. "There's
something wrong with him. He just sits all the time in
a wheelchair and watches television. Was it a man with
black hair and a toolbox that you saw?" he asked.

Patty nodded. "He just hurried by and didn't speak."

"Oh, that was the television repairman," Elwood
said. "Mr. Penny is always having his set fixed—he's
awful fussy about it. Anyway I'd never suspect Mrs.
Penny. She's always giving Bluebell some little treat
and is real kind. Besides," he added, "I see their mail
when it comes. It's mostly from California."

Just then Bluebell began to clang loudly on her bell.

Patty took her some peanuts, locking the tower room when she returned.

"I just thought of something, Elwood," she said. "You remember when we first came you suspected *us* —because Daddy looked like one of those cousins you saw in a picture?"

Elwood nodded.

"Are there any more old pictures around here?"

"Sure. There are lots of them down in the basement with Mrs. Truelove's things. There are old books and letters, too. I helped Pa store them."

Patty's pretty, pixielike face shone with interest. "Why don't we go down there and check over those pictures?" she suggested. "We might find some interesting evidence."

"They're awfully old," said Elwood, "taken years ago."

He got to his feet, however, and so did Scott. Scott was intrigued by Patty's plan but, as usual, he was more cautious.

"Do you think it's right to go poking around among Mrs. Truelove's things?" he asked.

"We'll go ask Pa if we can," said Elwood. "Mrs. True-love left him in charge of everything."

They wasted no time in hunting up Mr. Hunch. He was at the carriage house mending a plank in the wide door.

His eyes twinkled when Elwood made his request.

"Why don't you go ask Miss Bluebell?" he suggested. "After all, she's the heiress."

They dutifully trooped back upstairs and asked Bluebell's permission to examine the personal effects of the former owner of the Tower Arms. They took the small monkey's answering chatter for consent, and were soon headed for the basement.

Elwood had brought a big flashlight, which he gave to Patty while he and Scott dragged a dusty trunk from a corner and shoved open the lid.

"Do you know the names of the seven cousins who will inherit this property?" Patty asked.

"Yep." Elwood reached into his pocket and handed Patty a piece of paper. He was a methodical investigator. "You'll notice there are four Truelove's, two Jacksons, and one cousin named Smith," he said. "I figure that if one of 'em is in this house, he's using an alias."

Patty studied the list by the light of the flashlight, and Scott looked over her shoulder. He read the names aloud: "Walter, Marjorie, Henrietta, and Winston Truelove; Mabel-Ruth and Carl Jackson; and Richard Smith."

He frowned, checking carefully over the list again. Suddenly, something struck him. "Listen," he cried. "'Carl Jackson'—what does that suggest to you?"

Elwood had been bending over the trunk, getting a pile of photographs. He handed part of them to Patty

as he looked up. "Carl Jackson," he repeated. His long face lit up. "Why, sure—he has the same initials as Caleb Jones! They could be the same person."

Scott nodded. "I've read somewhere that when criminals take an assumed name, they often choose one with their real initials. Of course this could be a coincidence."

"It's mighty odd, all the same," said Elwood flatly.

The photographs were very old. Many were of Mrs. Truelove and her husband when they were young. Some were of children.

"Which one did you think looked like Daddy?" Patty asked.

Elwood rifled through his stack of pictures. He held out one of a dark-haired infant in a long christening dress. Patty stared at it and began to laugh.

"Why, this baby doesn't look any more like Daddy than you do!"

"Well, it has a cleft chin," the boy said stubbornly.

"So does Scott," Patty scoffed. "So does Caleb—"

She stopped talking and slowly turned the baby picture over. On the back, in faded ink, was the notation "Carl Jackson—six months old." She read it out loud.

"Poor Mr. Jones," she murmured before Elwood could say a word.

Beyond the cleft chins, they found little help in the pictures. There was one of a fat baby who might have been Mrs. Penny sixty years before. But it could have been any one of a million other people, too. There was another of a scrawny little girl of about seven, who looked faintly like Miss Twittengale. However, the name on the back of that one was Caroline Ridout, and *she* wasn't even one of the seven cousins.

Disappointed, Patty turned to a pile of letters which Elwood handed her. They were mostly from Mrs. Truelove's son and were the usual messages of a man to his mother, telling about his business and his family.

In one he described his small daughter. ". . . You'll love Claretta, Mom," the letter said. "She looks exactly like that beautiful Swede I married, and is a little blue-eyed cherub."

Patty found a small white Bible in the trunk, with the names of the family in it and the dates of their births; after each one was penciled a tiny question mark.

Then she found a baby book, in which Mrs. Truelove had kept a record of her son's life in the old house. It contained a tinted photograph of a fair-haired, blue-eyed boy and the usual records of his height and weight.

After both Scott and Elwood had examined these books, Patty put them back among the relics in the trunk.

"It must have been a great tragedy for Mrs. Truelove when her son and his family were lost at sea," she said sadly.

"Well, it happened over fifteen years ago," said Elwood, "so I don't remember, of course. But Pa knew

Mrs. Truelove's son real well, and he even saw the little girl once, when she visited here."

"Didn't they search for the family?" asked Scott.

"Oh, yes. Mrs. Truelove spent a lot of money and offered big rewards. She hoped some ship had picked them up, or that they had gotten to an island and would come back sometime. Pa thinks that is why Mrs. Truelove wrote such a funny will leaving everything to Bluebell," added Elwood. "She still hoped her son might come back."

"Not much chance after fifteen years," Scott remarked.

"Nope." Elwood slammed the lid of the trunk down and he and Scott shoved it back against the basement wall. "But maybe somebody whose real name is Carl Jackson has turned up."

The three turned to leave. Then Patty gave a little screech. And Scott all but jumped out of his skin.

Standing in the middle of the cellar floor—as though he had sprung magically from nowhere in answer to the name of Carl Jackson—was Caleb Jones himself!

Elwood glowered. "What are you doing here—spying on us?"

The artist's dark mood of the morning had changed completely. "Spying?" he repeated. "My dear boy, I was just looking for all of you to impart some great news. My painting has won first prize in the art show!"

He was so excited his voice cracked. His face could only be described as shining.

For a moment the three just stared at him, filled as they were with the guilty knowledge that Bluebell had had an important part in creating the masterpiece.

Then Scott found his voice. "That's great, Mr. Jones," he said warmly. "Congratulations!"

"It's wonderful," agreed Patty.

Even Elwood was generous enough to withhold his unkind thoughts from the artist, but he continued to regard Caleb with open suspicion.

"The show opens tomorrow, promptly at one o'clock," declared Caleb. "I want to invite you all to come."

"We will," promised Scott. He had been reading about a famous collection of jewelry that was to be shown at the Gem and Mineral Show, and he was very anxious to see it. Also he was thinking that this was the *third* time that the artist had reminded him of the exhibition.

"You, too, Elwood," Caleb added magnanimously. "I extend to you my special invitation."

"I was coming anyway," Elwood stated. "I want to study the meteorites they're going to have on display."

His lack of interest was lost on the artist, and Caleb went off happily. "I must tell the other tenants," he said. "I want everyone in Tower Arms to be there."

When he had gone, the three young people looked at each other in confusion. "Do you think he's on the level?" Scott asked. "He's making a lot of fuss about that picture."

"Well, it is pretty important to win first prize," said Patty, "but it's funny the way he insists that everybody go to the art show. Do you suppose he just wants to get us all out of the house so he can make another attempt to steal Bluebell?"

"That's it," said Elwood triumphantly. "I knew he was the one. Well, I'll fool him. I won't go to his old show at all."

"That's silly, Elwood," said Patty. "You want to see those rocks and minerals, too. Why don't we all go and just take Bluebell along? Then we'll know she's safe."

"I don't think we'll be allowed to bring a monkey into the auditorium," put in Scott. "They probably have rules about it."

"Oh, she can't hurt anything," Patty said confidently. "You just leave it all to me. Bluebell obeys me and never gets into mischief when I take care of her. I'll work it out so that nobody but us will even know she's there."

8

Something Bright and Shiny

DESPITE HIS sister's promises, Scott Carter discovered the next afternoon that it wasn't quite as easy to disguise a mischievous monkey as Patty thought. The clothes were no problem. It was a cool and cloudy day, so the girl was able to hide Bluebell's hairy little limbs completely with long blue jeans and a sweater. A hat with a brim hid most of her face.

But the tail did present a problem. At first she tried coiling it up and tying it, but Miss Bluebell would have none of that. So Patty tucked it under the long sweater as best she could, and it stuck out behind in a peculiar fashion.

There was quite a crowd going into the basement of the big civic building where the show was being held. All went well at first. Patty led Bluebell by the hand and instructed Scott and Elwood to stay close at her heels so that no one would have a chance to observe too closely.

They had no trouble finding the art display. At one end of the enormous basement were tables covered with bright pottery and carved figures. On the walls were paintings of all sizes and styles. Beside some of them stood the proud artists.

Caleb Jones's familiar picture was well displayed right in the center. On its frame was a bright blue ribbon.

Scott caught a glimpse of Mrs. Penny and Miss Twittengale examining some pottery; and he knew that his parents and Elwood's father were around somewhere. But there was no sign of Caleb Jones himself.

"Will *he* get a shock when he goes up to Bluebell's attic and finds her gone!" Scott said with a laugh. He felt convinced now that Elwood's suspicions were correct. The artist had made sure that he would be alone at the Tower Arms.

There was quite an interest in Caleb Jones's prize picture. Some viewed it with obvious pleasure, others with frank puzzlement.

Bluebell showed no interest in the picture at all, despite the fact that she had been partly responsible for its success. When she became restless, Patty picked her up and held her like a baby.

Near them was a little girl standing behind her father's legs, sucking her thumb. When she looked up into Bluebell's face her eyes grew big. She took her thumb out of her mouth and seemed about to speak.

Patty jabbed Scott with her elbow. "Let's go look at

the Gem and Mineral Show," she said, moving quickly away.

Elwood had already drifted off, and they found him at a table watching a lapidary artist who was polishing agate. There were tumbling machines working, and many collections of rare rock specimens were displayed on counters. But the center of attraction was the famous Granada collection of precious gems.

The jewelry, set with glowing diamonds, rubies, and emeralds, was displayed in a glass case. It had apparently arrived late, for two uniformed guards had just come in with a strongbox, and a distinguished-looking

gentleman in a black suit was just lifting the last and
most famous piece of all—the "Gems of Heaven" necklace—from a nest of velvet in the box.

According to a little sign Scott was looking at, it had
once belonged to a Spanish queen, and it was worth
three hundred thousand dollars! In the artificial light
it sparkled like a string of twinkling stars.

Patty had come up beside the man in charge. As he
lifted the lovely thing there was a gasp of admiration
from the crowd. All eyes were on it, including Bluebell's. It was one of those bright and shiny things she
loved.

Without warning, she suddenly leaped from Patty's
careless arms, landed for a split second on the man's
shoulder, snatched the necklace—and was off. Over the
case, through the astounded crowd of onlookers, she
headed for the stairway.

Patty screamed. The distinguished-looking gentleman could only manage a strangled gasp. The two
guards shouted angrily as they tried to follow the
swift-moving Bluebell.

No one but Patty and Scott really knew what had
happened.

Unfortunately when Bluebell reached the exit, a
whole troop of Brownie Scouts was just coming in.
They courteously held the door open for the escaping
thief. So when Patty and Scott and Elwood came charg-
ing up the steps—followed by the distraught gentleman, followed by the frantic guards, followed by the

excited crowd—the happy Brownies stood like a dam before a flood.

By the time the pursuers had untangled themselves and found another exit, Bluebell had scampered over the tops of seventeen cars, through half a dozen trees, and was on the top of a building two blocks away. She had lost her hat, and when Scott caught a glimpse of her, she was scratching her hairy little head with one hand and holding the necklace up with the other.

The sun was hidden behind a dense gray cloud and perhaps the gems didn't gleam as brightly as they had under the lights. The monkey swung them back and forth.

"Why it's a monkey!" shouted someone in the crowd.

"Bluebell," screamed Patty, "come down from there."

"*This instant,*" screamed the distinguished-looking gentleman from beside her, losing his dignity and shaking his fist.

Bluebell looked down at him over the edge of the building, making a smacking sound with her lips. One of the guards pulled out his gun.

"Don't shoot her," cried Elwood.

"No, indeed!" The custodian of the gem collection shoved the guard aside. "She might fling the jewels into some cranny we couldn't get at. We have to use strategy. . . . Come down, little fellow," he wheedled. "I'll give you some nice peanuts."

Meanwhile the two guards dashed around behind the building to find a way up to the roof. Scott, Patty, and Elwood just looked at each other and shook their heads. Then, as they feared, Bluebell looked behind her and saw the uniformed figures sneaking up on her. She hopped across the roof and made a lightning leap to the next building.

Once started, she kept on going, to the consternation of the followers. Half the time they couldn't see her as they ran shouting through the streets of Lincoln. But they caught glimpses of her—in the trees, on a church steeple.

"Bluebell's trying to get home," Scott gasped to Patty. They were both breathless from running. "Let's head for the Tower Arms." And the custodian, the guards, and the growing mob, having no other leaders, followed Patty, Elwood, and Scott. Even Mr. and Mrs. Carter had joined in the chase, as confused by it all as the others.

Just as Scott had anticipated, they found Miss Bluebell at home. She was waiting on the window ledge outside her own room in the tower. As Scott came up below, she gravely put the priceless jewels around her neck. Then she turned and tried to open the window.

"I think she'll stay there for now," remarked Scott. "That's where she lives and she won't feel secure till she gets inside."

"I don't care about her security," panted the representative for the Granada gem collection. "I'm interested in the security of those jewels. What do we do now?"

Scott looked at Elwood. "Why can't we go up to the tower room and coax her inside from there? I think it might work."

Elwood shook his head glumly. "Can't open those windows," he said. "When Miss Bluebell's apartment was fixed up, that heavy screen inside was put on solid. By the time we could cut it, she would get suspicious and take off again."

Meanwhile Patty was pleading with Bluebell to come to her. The monkey was chattering back a shrill refusal. The two guards were blundering around helplessly, not knowing what to do. And various onlookers were making clever suggestions.

"Why doesn't somebody get up there on the tower with a net and drop it over the monkey?" said one man. Nobody bothered to answer that.

"Get a bag of peanuts," suggested fat little Mrs. Penny, who had finally arrived, puffing and wheezing, and was standing near Scott. "The dear little thing loves peanuts."

"I'll go home and get my lasso," said a tall man from the rear of the crowd. "I was a cowhand for thirty years. Ain't a livin' creature I can't rope with my lasso."

That was the best suggestion yet. Everyone waited anxiously while the man got his lasso. Mr. Hunch showed him how to get on the roof of the old house. Then, with a hundred pairs of eyes watching every move, the man took a precarious perch on a projecting gable. He swung the rope slowly around his head.

But Miss Bluebell had been watching him too. The instant the old cowboy tossed the rope the monkey scrambled around to the other side of the tower. The cowboy took a new position and tried again, but the agile monkey was too fast for him. He finally had to admit defeat.

Strangely enough, it was Caleb Jones who made the most sensible suggestion. He came out of the big house and made his way around the excited crowd to where Scott stood beside Elwood.

"What's all the fuss about?" he asked.

The worried boys explained what had happened, forgetting in the stress of the moment their recent suspicion of the artist.

"I was looking for my green-striped shirt—getting ready to go down to the civic center—when I heard all the commotion," said Caleb. He looked up at Miss Bluebell, still clinging to her perch on the tower. "Where I come from we always call the fire department. They know what to do in cases like this."

"Somebody ring them!" cried the man in black, who by now had a wild gleam in his eye.

So the fire department came to the rescue. The hook-and-ladder truck roared up with a shrilling of sirens, followed by the fire chief's car. He was followed by several reporters and two photographers, who had by now gotten wind of the fabulous theft.

A gang of firemen came up to survey the situation. After a conference with the chief, they moved the crowd of onlookers out of the yard. Then the fire truck carefully backed up to the tower. A long ladder rose magically against the background of the gray sky, then leaned toward the tower where Bluebell waited.

She curled her lower lip and hissed as it came close. One of the firemen climbed up the ladder to bring Bluebell down. But of course when he reached for her, she was no longer there. She caught the ledge above the window and moved to the weathervane at the top of the conical tower.

The fireman came down shaking his head. Another one made the same attempt, climbing out on the ledge of the window. Bluebell took off the necklace and swung it around, just out of his reach. The man came down to confer with his chief.

"She doesn't trust them," Scott said with a sigh, looking hopelessly at Elwood.

Elwood turned to Patty, who was almost in tears. "Let *her* go up the ladder," he said to the firemen. "If Bluebell will go to anyone, it's Patty. She loves her."

The fireman looked at Patty's small, eager face.

"*Please*," she begged.

"It's too risky," said the chief.

"I'm not scared. I've climbed to plenty of places higher than that. Haven't I, Mother?" She spoke challengingly to Mrs. Carter, who now stood nearby with a doubtful look on her face.

"Certainly she has." Patty's father spoke up. "She

climbs like a mountain goat. Let her go up and coax that animal down."

Finally the chief agreed to the plan, as long as Patty's parents consented.

So Patty climbed the long ladder with the fire chief right behind her. The onlookers held their breath.

"Come on, Bluebell," pleaded Patty, near the top of the ladder. "Let's go get some peanuts!"

She held out her arms to the little monkey. Bluebell drew back, scolding saucily. Then she changed her mind, came down almost within reach of Patty's fingers —but scampered away again.

Again and again Patty tried to coax the small creature from the roof.

"It's no use," said the chief.

Then suddenly, when even Patty was in despair, a small miracle occurred. The sun came out from behind the clouds. A bright ray of sunshine struck Patty's blond head and turned her hair to shining gold.

The gleam of her curls was more entrancing than the glittering necklace. With a rapturous squeal and a small leap, Miss Bluebell landed on the top rung of the ladder and buried her hairy little hands in those curls.

A flashbulb flared as a photographer snapped a picture. And a few minutes later the costly Gems of Heaven were back in the hands of the embarrassed guards.

"We'd better take Bluebell back to her apartment," said Patty, "before she gets away from us again. She's too excited now."

"That's just what somebody around here would like," said Elwood. "If she ran off and never came back." His face was still white from the strain and worry of the little monkey's escape.

Scott looked warily around. Dozens of curious eyes were staring at Bluebell. That "somebody" might be one of these very people—even a stranger.

9

The New Tenant

No DOUBT about it, Miss Bluebell was a celebrity. Reporters came from as far away as Kansas City and Omaha to interview her. She appeared with Elwood and Patty on the *Morning Show* on television. The pictures of Patty climbing the fire ladder in front of the Truelove mansion to retrieve the Gems of Heaven appeared in half the newspapers in the land.

In all the excitement, the three young investigators might have been distracted from their anxiety over Bluebell's welfare if Scott hadn't made a disturbing discovery. The very day after the jewel theft, he happened to drop his fountain pen in front of the attic door. When he stooped to pick it up, he found some tiny scrapings of wax on the floor.

Elwood examined the particles, and his long face grew longer. "Somebody made a wax impression of this lock," he declared. "They'll have a key made from it."

"It must have happened yesterday while we were

gone," said Patty with conviction. "And it must have been Caleb Jones. He had a perfect chance to do it while we were at the art show. And if he has a key he can get into the attic whenever he wants to!"

The very thought was alarming. Caleb Jones was a perfect suspect. But they were to discover that he wasn't the only one in Tower Arms. They found new cause for worry in the person of Miss Twittengale.

Mrs. Carter had arranged for Patty to take a few lessons from the music teacher and to practice in her apartment. It was while Patty was doing exercises on the ancient piano that Miss Twittengale made her strange remark.

"This piano is so old it's difficult to keep in tune. I hope to buy a new one before long. In fact—" she lowered her voice as though imparting a secret—"I expect to come into *quite* a sum of money one of these days."

"Where would *she* get a lot of money?" Elwood asked anxiously when Patty told him what she had heard.

"Maybe we should keep an eye on her as well as on Caleb Jones," said Patty. "She could be one of Mrs. Truelove's cousins."

"For all we know," said Scott, "the house is full of them!"

Under the circumstances, they decided to talk to Elwood's father. Now even the trusting Mr. Hunch seemed impressed.

"Does look a mite funny," he admitted. "Of course,

if Miss Bluebell just up and disappeared, the court would have to give the house and money to the nearest heir or heirs, like the will says. Still . . ." He scratched his head. "We can't order all our tenants to leave just because we found a little scrap of wax on the floor.

"Tell you what, Elwood," he went on. "Might be a good idea for you to move your bed up there in the attic so's you can keep an eye on Bluebell at night. And don't leave her with anybody you can't trust for sure."

Elwood moved his cot to the attic. Patty and Scott did their part by keeping watch over the little heiress when Elwood was busy with his chores or doing one of his scientific experiments.

Patty had fun playing house in the attic. She kept the rooms tidy, washed Bluebell's clothes, and often fed her. The affectionate little animal adored her.

For a while life at the Tower Arms settled into a peaceful routine. Caleb Jones got busy on another masterpiece. Miss Twittengale's reluctant piano students came and went. The Pennys' television set broke down a few times, bringing the repairman to the house quite regularly. But Mrs. Penny found time to make a red flannel coat for Bluebell, with bright brass buttons and a special pocket for peanuts.

On Saturdays, when Mr. Carter was free, the family often went sight-seeing—driving over the checkered prairie, or picnicking at a pleasant spot along the river. Now and then Elwood and his father joined them when

Mr. Hunch was willing to interrupt his work and whistling for a few hours.

Bluebell always joined these happy outings, sticking her small face out of the car window, like a contented family dog, to breathe the sweet air.

One afternoon when they returned from such a picnic they found a newcomer at the Tower Arms. A strange young woman was sitting on the porch talking with Mrs. Penny. She was waiting for Mr. Hunch, and she wanted to rent an apartment.

Scott Carter thought that he had never seen a prettier young woman in his life. She looked about twenty.

She had lovely dark blond hair and dewy brown eyes. When she asked Mr. Hunch about the apartment she spoke in a soft, hesitant voice, with an accent new to Scott. She said her name was Linda Blake.

"Yes, siree, Miss Blake," said Mr. Hunch. "Number six is vacant—right across from the Carters on the third floor."

He turned and introduced them all around, and when Mr. Hunch led the newcomer up the stairs, the Carter family followed with their picnic baskets.

"It will be nice to have a neighbor right across the hall," remarked Mrs. Carter when they were back in number five.

"Especially such a young and pretty one," said Mr. Carter, handing a thermos jug to Scott to take to the kitchen. "I wonder why she picked an old house like this."

Scott and Patty wondered too. And they were more curious than ever when Miss Linda Blake went away and returned again in a taxi with just two small suitcases.

They found out a little more about the new tenant a few minutes later when plump Mrs. Penny knocked on the door. She had come to bring some freshly baked bread—and also to gossip a bit, Scott soon decided.

"Can't stay but a minute," she insisted, settling into the cherrywood love seat. "It's odd, though, about that Miss Blake," she went right on, to Mrs. Carter. "Why would a single young woman want a big apartment like that? She's just new in town, too. Has a job at the Parfait Sweet Shop—can't make much money there."

"Perhaps she just wants a quiet place to stay," Mrs. Carter said gently. Then they all laughed together.

"*Quiet?*" said Scott. "She won't get much quiet with Bluebell around!"

"Well, it seems mighty peculiar to me," insisted Mrs. Penny, not to be distracted. "She told me she's been working in New York—modeling dresses for teen-agers in a department store. Why would she want to leave the big city to come out to the prairie?"

"Many people do, Mrs. Penny," said Scott's mother, looking somewhat annoyed. "Including the Carters. We like it here."

When their visitor had gone, Mrs. Carter looked around at her family. "Since this is her first night at the Tower Arms, and Miss Blake won't have any food on hand, why don't we invite her for supper? Of course it won't be fancy, after the huge picnic lunch we had, but—"

The family agreed wholeheartedly. Patty and Scott raced each other across the hall to extend the invitation.

Their new neighbor was grateful and very happy to come. She seemed to enjoy the peppery goulash which Mrs. Carter prepared.

"It is delicious," she said. She pronounced the short *i* like *ee*, and said del*ee*cious.

With her next words they understood why. "We used

much hot chili pepper in our food when I was a little girl," she said. "I was born in Mexico."

"That's why you were named Linda," said Patty eagerly. "It means 'pretty,' doesn't it?"

The girl nodded, her swift smile making her very pretty indeed. "My name was Linda Rodriguez," she told them, "but when I was eleven, some people brought me to New York and adopted me. So now I am Linda Blake."

"Are you really adopted?" Patty was gazing at the older girl in wonder. She thought it very romantic to be adopted.

"Yes, really," said Linda. But she didn't seem to want to talk about it any more, and changed the subject rather abruptly.

"Tell me about the little monkey, Patty," she said instead. "I saw you with it downstairs."

"Oh, that's Miss Bluebell," said Patty, laughing. And she was off on a tale of what was now her favorite subject—the antics, both funny and disgraceful, of Bluebell. Linda was entranced by the story. But when Patty began to describe the fairy-tale apartment in the attic, her listener's face grew suddenly serious.

"You must take me up to see it, Patty," she broke in. And she said it so intensely that Scott found himself staring at her.

"I'll take you tomorrow," promised Patty. "It will be Sunday and you won't have to work."

"We'll ask Elwood," Scott said, cautious as usual. He remembered Elwood's unfriendly reception when the Carters had arrived at the Tower Arms. So far, Scott liked Miss Blake, but he knew that Elwood might not be so easily won.

He was right. When Patty made the suggestion the next morning, Elwood shook his head and scowled.

"I don't trust Miss Blake," he said. "She asked Pa and me a lot of busybody questions about this place, and she paid only two weeks' rent in advance, instead of for a month."

"Maybe that's all the money she had," said Patty in quick defense.

"There's more." Elwood went on as if Patty hadn't spoken. "After I went to bed last night I heard her go into the hall. I got dressed and kept an eye on her, and she was sure acting funny. Wandered all over the first and second floors of the house—even peeked into the broom closet!"

Patty frowned. They were all up in Bluebell's apartment, and she was peeling a banana for the monkey. Bluebell was beside her, begging plaintively for her to hurry.

"I suppose Linda was just looking her new home over, Elwood," Patty said finally, glancing up at the tall boy. "She simply *couldn't* be one of the seven cousins. She's too young, and besides that, she's too *nice*."

"She could be the daughter of one of them," Elwood

retorted ominously. "She didn't come to the Tower Arms just by chance, Patty Carter. You can bank on that."

Secretly Scott had to agree. Like Patty, he too was impressed with the attractive young tenant in number six. But she was behaving in a very strange manner.

10

Bluebell Gives a Party

WITH THE coming of Miss Linda Blake the cloud of suspicion that had hovered over the old house became thicker than ever.

Linda herself was lovely. She had beautiful manners and was sweet and gracious to everyone. She did kind, thoughtful things for all the tenants. She invited Patty and Scott down to the Parfait Sweet Shop where she worked and treated them to luscious concoctions with extra scoops of ice cream.

Nevertheless, even Scott felt there was something suspicious about Linda. For one thing, she kept trying to wheedle her way into the attic to look around. For another, she was too curious about the old Truelove property, and Scott often spied her wandering around the grounds, peeping into the cellar windows or into the carriage house.

On top of that, she was very friendly with Caleb Jones, taking a great interest in his painting. They took

walks together, and in the evenings they chatted together in low voices in the swing on the porch.

"They've known each other before," Elwood remarked darkly. Other odd things happened, too.
Bluebell had another bout of tummy ache, and Miss
Twittengale had been seen taking another of her odd
excursions in the upper hall. Finally the three amateur
sleuths had a conference in the attic.

"I agree there's something fishy going on," said
Scott. "Maybe your father should send Miss Bluebell
away to a boarding kennel for pets for a while, Elwood," he suggested. "Then if there is somebody in
this house who has been trying to kidnap her, he or she
will go away."

Elwood shook his head. "That would break the will,"
he said. "Miss Bluebell is supposed to live right here in
this house."

Patty's blue eyes were thoughtful. She was still loyal
to her beloved Linda, but she wanted to protect Bluebell.

"I have an idea," she said suddenly. "Why can't we
set a trap for the guilty person? Let me think . . . Bluebell could give a party, and we can invite all the tenants in the Tower Arms."

"What kind of trap is that?" Scott laughed.

"Well, maybe one of them would give himself
away—"

"I know," Elwood interrupted. "We can invite them
all, and then say, just offhand like, that we are going

to paint and spray up here and we have to move Bluebell's bed out to the carriage house for a couple of
nights. There isn't any lock on it, you know."

"Then," Patty burst in, "we can hide in there, and
whoever it is will think Bluebell is alone and will come
and try to take her. When they know we've found them
out, they'll be scared off."

It was an exciting idea. They knew that it might not
work and that whoever was trying to make trouble
might not fall for the tempting bait, but it was worth
a try. Mr. Hunch agreed to let them carry it out, and
Mr. Carter agreed that Scott, but not Patty, might hide
in the carriage house with Elwood to corner the culprit
—provided that one of the men was hidden nearby.

The invitations were extended immediately. Patty
invited Linda Blake and told Miss Twittengale about
the party when she went to take her lesson. Elwood
grudgingly invited Caleb Jones, and Scott himself was
appointed to go see Mrs. Penny.

She was delighted when he knocked on the door of
number four and told her Bluebell was giving a party.

"I'll furnish part of the refreshments," she offered
happily. "I'll make cupcakes."

"That will be grand," said Scott. He looked past her
into the living room where Mr. Penny was sitting in
front of the television set in his wheelchair. He could
just see the man's arm and hand and the top of his gray
head.

"I hope Mr. Penny will come too," Scott added. "I'll

be glad to wheel his chair out, and Elwood and I can take him upstairs."

Mrs. Penny smiled her sweet smile. "We'll see how he feels, Scott. I know he'd like to come, but he doesn't get around much, you know."

From then on preparations for the party went full speed ahead. Patty and Scott had so much fun they almost forgot the serious purpose of the celebration. And Bluebell herself was just as excited by it all.

Elwood brought several dozen bright balloons for decoration. Patty made twelve fancy paper caps, one for everyone, including Miss Bluebell. Mrs. Carter made two gallons of punch and three dozen tiny party sandwiches. Mrs. Penny brought her cupcakes, and even Bluebell helped.

Mr. Hunch found an old-fashioned ice-cream churn in the basement. Patty and her mother mixed the vanilla and custard. Elwood furnished the crushed ice and salt. And Bluebell, crouched on the floor of the attic, turned the freezer.

It was quite a party. Everybody came but Mr. Penny, and he sent his regrets. They all sat on the tiny furniture or on the floor, wearing their funny hats, and ate up all the delicious food. Miss Twittengale contributed her share to the festivities by playing Bluebell's toy piano and singing in her sweet, cracked voice. The guests joined in. Bluebell did her acrobatic tricks and shook hands agreeably with everyone when they left— except Caleb Jones.

They all had such a good time that even Elwood almost forgot to lay the trap. Then, just as the guests were leaving, Patty spoke up.

"It's a good thing Bluebell gave her party tonight," she said so clearly that everyone stopped to listen. "Tomorrow Elwood's going to move everything out and start painting and spraying up here."

"Spraying?" Mrs. Penny looked dismayed. "That might be dangerous for Bluebell."

"Oh, we aren't going to leave her here," Elwood explained. "We're going to move her bed out to the carriage house until we have her apartment ready again. She'll be all right out there."

"The carriage house?" This echo was from Linda, who had been taking a last survey of the attic. There was a dreamy, faraway expression in her brown eyes.

Maybe she's dreaming of the Truelove fortune, Scott thought. And suddenly he felt deflated. He hated to uncover anything bad about the tenants of the Tower Arms. Just now they all seemed so friendly—so nice.

The next day Elwood set up the trap. He brought some cans of paint up to the attic to make it look like business. Then he and Scott carried Bluebell's small bed down to the carriage house and put it in the corner. That night, after dark, they took Bluebell into the old building and she jumped right onto her bed. Just to be on the safe side, they put on her harness and leash and snapped it to a hook on the wall nearby.

They openly went back into the big house, then sneaked down into the basement and out the cellar door to slip into the carriage house for the night. Elwood hid in the big sedan. Scott crept into the old electric car and settled down to listen.

For a while Bluebell made quite a fuss, chattering and whimpering and showing plainly that she disapproved of these new arrangements. But finally she settled down and went to sleep. Scott leaned back in a corner of the leather seat. The ancient car smelled musty.

He looked at the radiant dial of his watch. It was exactly ten o'clock.

Then he dozed off, his chin on his chest. He came awake with a jerk, startled by a faint, creaking noise.

The old plank door was slowly moving on its hinges. Somebody was coming into the trap!

From where Scott sat in the old car, he could just see the top of the opening widen. Then he heard scraping footsteps inside the building. A flashlight was snapped on, and someone moved stealthily across the floor.

But that someone was not moving toward the corner where Bluebell slept. The light was coming straight to the antique car where Scott was hiding.

The car door finally opened and light splashed over Scott's face. Then—all in one instant—a girl screamed, the flashlight fell, and Elwood Hunch shouted: "Stop right there, Miss Linda Blake!"

The noise woke Bluebell, and she began a fearsome chatter. Linda, more startled than anyone, ran pell-mell for the door.

11

A Strange Story

WHEN ELWOOD AND SCOTT dashed out of the carriage house, they fully expected to find Linda gone. But she was standing in the dark, waiting for them. She held her robe close about her.

"Oh, you *frightened* me, Scott Carter," she told him accusingly. "What were you doing—hiding in that old car at two o'clock in the morning?"

"The important question is, What were *you* doing in the carriage house?" Elwood demanded before Scott could reply.

Instead of taking offense, Linda Blake began to laugh, in a strange soft way. "I was looking for something, Elwood—something I lost . . . a long time ago."

"We—we thought you were after Bluebell," Scott said, feeling a little foolish. "We were there to protect her."

"Oh, no," the girl said. "I wouldn't harm Bluebell. I was looking for a little rag doll."

All at once she went between Scott and Elwood, back into the old building. With the puzzled boys at her heels, she groped her way to the electric car. Finding the flashlight, she snapped it on and climbed into the car—feeling all about between the frame and the seat.

Suddenly she gave a little cry of triumph. And backing down to the floor, she turned and held in the beam of the flashlight a tiny stuffed doll!

Just about that time Scott's father and Mr. Hunch came into the carriage house. They had been watching from a window.

"What's all the fuss about?" Mr. Hunch asked.

It was Scott who spoke up, in a puzzled voice. "I don't know, but I think Linda has been here before."

"Yes," said the girl. She was dusting off the doll. "It was a long time ago, I was just a little girl. I wasn't sure this was the right house," she went on, "it has been changed so. But when I went to the party in the attic tonight, I thought I'd been in it before; and when somebody mentioned 'carriage house,' I got to thinking. . . ."

"About what?" said Scott when she stopped talking.

"About a doll I lost when I was sitting in this car with a dear old lady. Then I remembered. I was cross and I stuffed it behind the seat. So tonight I felt I couldn't wait until morning to come and see if it was here."

"Then *you* must be Mrs. Truelove's lost granddaughter!" Elwood gasped.

"I don't know," Linda said in a dazed way. "I saw a picture of this old house in the newspaper—there was an article about it, telling all about the little monkey and how she had stolen that necklace and inherited this house. I cut the clipping out and kept looking at it. I just had a feeling I had seen the house before. . . . I don't know why, but I just *had* to come and find out."

"Well, this is mighty unexpected," said Mr. Hunch. "But I think you better not talk about it any more tonight."

"I agree," said Scott's father quietly. "You should

go back to your room and rest, Linda. We can discuss all this in the morning. Come on, Scott."

Scott was disappointed. He wanted to hear the rest of Linda's story. At the moment he was more confused than enlightened by this new phase in the Truelove mystery. Where had the girl been all these years? Was she really the heiress, or was she an imposter?

Bluebell was cutting up now, whistling and jabbering because she had been disturbed. Elwood got her and took her back to the attic with him. It seemed unlikely that anyone else would walk into the trap after all the commotion.

Scott followed his father, who led the seemingly dazed Linda back upstairs. When they passed the second-floor landing, he was surprised to see Caleb Jones standing in the hallway fully dressed. Caleb looked as though he wanted to ask some questions, but Scott went right on. He was too absorbed in his own thoughts to worry about the suspicious Caleb just then.

In the morning Elwood came around to fill Scott in on the rest of Linda's strange story. She had talked again to Mr. Hunch before she left for work.

After a night of scientific reasoning, Elwood was his usual doubting self. Patty and Mrs. Carter had heard about the lost-and-found doll by now and were both bursting to hear more. So Mrs. Carter made Elwood a stack of pancakes and poured him some milk, and they all sat at the table while Elwood told Linda's story.

"Linda *says* she's from Mexico," he began, generously pouring syrup over his pancakes. "It was somewhere in Baja California, and she lived with a Mexican family."

"And their name was Rodriguez," said Patty eagerly. "That's what she told us."

"Yes, she thought they were her own people and that her name was really Linda Rodriguez."

"But how did she come to be there?" asked Mrs. Carter.

"She doesn't know. Or so she says." Elwood paused thoughtfully for another mouthful of pancake. "She remembers living in a little adobe hut. She remembers helping her Mexican mother make tortillas. But that's all—she doesn't know anything that happened before that."

"How did she come to be adopted by the Blake family?" Scott took his turn asking a question.

"Well, this American couple came down there about ten years ago on a vacation. Mr. Blake is a businessman in New York, and that part of Mexico is wild country, with hardly any roads, so they must have been adventurous. They saw Linda, I guess, and liked her and brought her back home with them. That's the way she tells it."

"It does seem strange," said Mrs. Carter thoughtfully as she poured more milk in Elwood's glass. "Why would her own family just give her away like that?"

"Because she wasn't really theirs, that's why," declared Patty with a romantic glow in her blue eyes. "The Rodriguez family must have rescued her from the sea, and they knew she wasn't Mexican, with her light hair and all, and they had no right to keep her—"

"Knock it off, Pat," said Scott. "You don't know a thing about it." He turned to Elwood. "Do you believe Linda's story?" he asked.

"No," said Elwood. "It's too vague. I think Linda Blake just read those stories in the paper—about Bluebell's fortune, and how Mrs. Truelove's son and his family were lost. She made all this Mexican business up and she's going to try to prove she's the real heiress."

"But what about the doll?" said Patty instantly. "She went right to it in that old car. Scott told me all about that. How did she know it was there?"

Elwood had done a lot of thinking. "She has accomplices, that's how," he said. "She probably has a crooked father in the East who will swear to all that stuff about her being from Mexico. And she has somebody right here in this house, who could have *planted* that doll in the old electric car.

"And you know who it could be," he added. "Somebody by the name of Caleb Jones, *or* Carl Jackson. He and Linda might even be related. Maybe they plan to get the whole fortune away from the other cousins."

"That could be," Scott admitted. "But I don't think

so, Elwood. Linda may be telling the truth, and if she *is* the real heiress, the court will give her Mrs. Truelove's money, isn't that right?"

"Yep." Elwood nodded. "There isn't any doubt about that. Pa talked to the lawyer on the phone about it this morning. But—" he looked up defiantly—"first she has to *prove* she's old Mrs. Truelove's granddaughter. How's she going to do that?"

12

Secrets from the Past

SCOTT AND PATTY knew that Elwood was right. Linda Blake would have to prove that she was really the lost Claretta before she could inherit the Truelove fortune.

Mr. Hunch's lawyer had been very emphatic about that. The question was, How was she going to prove such a fantastic story?

The next day was Sunday. Mrs. Carter, feeling sorry for the troubled girl, asked her to attend church with the family. They brought her back with them to dinner.

She wore a pink linen suit which Scott thought looked very pretty with her dark golden hair and brown eyes. Patty brought her an apron and she helped Mrs. Carter make the salad.

"The human memory is a mysterious thing," Mr. Carter remarked as he carved the roast. "You must have been a very young child, Linda, when you visited this old house, yet the impression was so strong you recognized it from a newspaper picture."

"Yes," Linda said, "if I *am* Claretta Truelove, I was only about five. Mr. Hunch remembers when the family came to this house."

"The strangest thing," said Patty, who was completely entranced by the latest turn of events, "is how she remembered where that little doll was."

Scott nodded, but he didn't say anything. He wondered about that himself. It seemed unnatural to him that somebody would remember a silly rag doll and not recall a single thing about a terrible shipwreck later.

Elwood made the same point later that afternoon. The two boys had brought Bluebell's bed back to the attic and Patty was putting a tightly fitted sheet on the small mattress.

"I think you're a mean, suspicious person, Elwood," Patty said. "After all the sweet things Linda has done around here, you just haven't any right to distrust her."

Elwood looked troubled, but he stood stubbornly silent.

"You're not being very scientific about this thing," Scott reminded him. "A real scientist waits till all the facts are in before drawing conclusions. Maybe you just don't want the real heiress to this house to turn up because you might have to move away from here . . . and lose Bluebell," he added accusingly.

Now Elwood looked absolutely miserable. He slowly shook his shock of yellow hair. "It isn't that at all, Scott," he answered. "Sure I'd hate to lose Bluebell, and I've

lived here all my life; but if Linda really owns the
Tower Arms, I want her to have it."

"What's eating you, then?"

"I don't know. I can't figure it out myself." The boy
looked earnestly at his two friends. "There's something
wrong about that girl—something that just doesn't add
up. I've thought and thought, and I can't figure out
what it is. . . . I just have a—a feeling."

"Elwood Hunch and his hunches," scoffed Patty.

Scott smiled at that, but he had no more to say. The
uncomfortable truth was that despite his argument
with Elwood, he understood the other boy's position.
There *was* something odd about Linda, or her story,
but he couldn't say what it was. Like Elwood he just
had a feeling that the girl couldn't possibly be the
missing Claretta. But why?

During the next few days, while the mystery smol-
dered, Elwood and his friends continued to guard
Bluebell. As far as they knew, she was still in danger
of being spirited away. They had told none of the
other tenants about Linda's strange story.

Elwood changed the lock on the attic door, so that
if a duplicate key *had* been made, it couldn't be used.
And the three friends took Bluebell with them when
they went adventuring.

One day they made the mistake of taking her to the
Parfait Sweet Shop, where Linda was working behind
the soda fountain. Patty offered to stay outside and
hold Bluebell on her leash while Scott and Elwood

went inside to buy ice-cream cones for all four of them.

While Patty was looking the other way, a customer came out of the shop, leaving the door open. Bluebell, in her best pink dress and bonnet, saw her chance. She darted through the door, dragging Patty after her.

Before Patty could stop her, the little monkey leaped onto a stool and pounded the counter, demanding service.

Linda had just set a huge Banana Special in front of a huge man in a checkered suit. The man lifted his spoon to scoop up the luscious cherry on top, but when he looked down, the cherry had vanished.

"Where's my cherry?" the man bellowed. Then he spied Bluebell's bonnet beside him. "This kid stole it!" he wailed. And when a small hairy arm shot out and pulled the entire Banana Special from under his nose, he jumped off the stool. Shaking all over, he ran out of the shop.

By that time Patty had caught the squirming monkey. The beautiful Banana Special was flying through the air—and the manager of the sweet shop came dashing out of the back room.

"No dogs allowed in this establishment," he shouted, pointing at Patty.

"She isn't a dog!" Patty shouted back.

The man took one look at Bluebell, then pointed to the door. "Out!" he screamed.

So Patty got out, and poor Linda, who was in no

way to blame, got a bawling out. Scott and Elwood left too, minus the four ice-cream cones.

Patty was cross with everybody. "I don't see why Linda works for that man," she said.

"She probably needs the money . . . and maybe she likes sweets," answered Scott reasonably.

"Everything she does is nuts," said Elwood, summing everything up in that one word, and they returned, hungry and out of sorts, to the Tower Arms.

At a suggestion from the lawyers, Linda finally wrote to the Blakes, telling them about her mysterious experience in the old house. She begged them to tell her all they could about her early years.

Her father's answer, which came by return mail, only added to the mystery. Linda brought the letter to the Carters' apartment and asked Scott to read it aloud.

My dear little girl:

To say that your mother and I were surprised at your strange news is to put it mildly. We never dreamed when we adopted you that you might be an American child and an heiress! In fact, we know little more about your infancy than you do.

The first time we ever saw you—as we have so often told you—was in a tiny remote village in Baja California, which your mother and I had discovered accidentally when we took a vagabond tour by jeep. You were just a barefooted tangle-haired waif, playing with some Mexican children, but we fell in love with your beautiful smile. You spoke not one word of English, and we thought you another fair-skinned child of the land.

Juan Rodriguez admitted to us that you were not his child but the child of his sister-in-law, and an orphan. When we begged him to let us take you back to the United States with us, he consented. He even produced papers telling where and when you were born. To us you were just another orphan, whom we wanted to love and to help. I realize now that we might have investigated further. At this late date I have wired my brother—your uncle Jim— in California, asking him to fly down to that village and question Juan again. I will let you know as soon as we find out more about your background.

Keep in touch, dear, and let us know if you need anything.

YOUR LOVING FATHER

"Now I don't know who I am," Linda said when Scott had finished. Her brown eyes were misty and her voice sad.

"But you know who you aren't," said Scott. "You are *not* Linda Rodriguez and never were. Maybe your Uncle Jim will find the answer when he gets to that little town."

The second letter was not long in coming. Elwood Hunch and his father joined Linda in the Carter living room to hear its amazing contents revealed.

Mr. Blake's brother had chartered a plane and flown to an airstrip near the coast of Baja California. From there he had taken a truck over mountain roads to the village—only to discover that Juan Rodriguez had moved away years before!

. . . I thought I had truly come on a wild goose chase, but when I began to inquire around in the village, I found that many people there remembered Linda. They called her *albinita*, which means "little white one" in Spanish; and *angelita*, which means "little angel." But they would not talk about her! I almost gave up, until I found a very old gray-haired woman, who had known Juan. She told me Juan Rodriguez' secret. It is a strange story, believe me.

It *was* a strange story, almost unbelievable, thought Scott when he had heard it. It was a story of a whole village, whose inhabitants had kept a dark secret for fifteen long years.

Juan Rodriguez was a very poor man, and sometimes he left his village and went down to the sea. There he would borrow a friend's boat and go fishing to get food for his family.

One day, while he was fishing, a terrible storm came over the sea and Juan was cast out into the waves. He fought for his life for many hours, and when he was about to give up and let himself sink, he saw something floating on the water near him. It was a big wooden box with rope handles. He paddled toward it and caught one of the handles and clung to it.

The box was not big enough for him to get into, but

when it rode on the swells of the water, he saw that something was inside already. He could not believe what he saw, and had to shake the salt sea from his eyes and look again.

It was a little girl with pale golden hair. She was tied inside the box, and was asleep. When she woke up, she smiled at him and didn't cry. Then Juan noticed something else. The storm was subsiding, and the wind, which a moment before had been cruel and wild, was now steadily but gently pushing the box toward shore.

Juan clung to the box and was saved. When he reached the shore, he took the little girl in his arms and carried her all the way back to the village. He told everyone about the miracle that had happened. He kept her with his own children and everyone in the village loved her and called her "little angel" because they thought she would bring them all good fortune.

Whenever anyone came from the outside world and asked questions about the little girl, the people of the village turned their heads and did not answer. They were afraid. And finally, the old woman said, two *norteamericanos* had come and taken the little angel away to another country.

No one in the Carter living room spoke after the story was revealed. Then Mr. Carter broke the silence.

"It all adds up," he said thoughtfully, looking at Linda, who was seated on the couch. "A family shipwrecked, a storm at sea—a little girl picked out of the

waves. And now, fifteen years later, a grown young woman walks into an old carriage house, which should have meant nothing to her, and goes right to her lost doll.

"There isn't much doubt in my mind," he added, "that Linda is really Claretta Truelove."

Linda looked at the faces around her. Her eyes were very dark in her white face.

"Now all she has to do is prove her claim," said Elwood.

Elwood was right. The lawyers were impressed with this new information, but they were not convinced that Linda was the granddaughter of old Mrs. Truelove. "It is circumstantial evidence," one of them had told Mr. Hunch, "but not proof. Miss Blake will need a lot more information than this to convince the court to set aside the will."

"Do you know where the real Claretta Truelove was born?" Mr. Carter asked Mr. Hunch later, after Linda had gone back to her room. "Did she have any identifying marks?"

Unfortunately Mr. Hunch did not know. "I wasn't working here when the little girl was born," he said.

Patty, who had been sitting by Scott, listening anxiously, popped suddenly to her feet.

"Maybe we could find out something about the baby in those old papers in the trunk," she suggested. "It's in the basement."

"We looked through all that junk," Elwood said heavily.

"Yes, but we didn't read *all* the letters," said Scott. "There were quite a few written by Mrs. Truelove's son and some of them mentioned the little girl."

He turned to his father. "Can't we go down right now and look, Dad?" he asked.

Mr. Carter glanced at his watch. "It's pretty late, Scott. But if Mr. Hunch says it's all right—"

"Sure thing," said Elwood's father. "I'd like to help that girl prove her case. If she is the heiress she has a lot more right to this property than those distant cousins. They never did like Mrs. Truelove—didn't even come to her funeral."

"Well, I don't want the children wandering down into that old dark place by themselves," said Mrs.

Carter, beginning to gather up glasses. "You men will have to go with them."

So Mr. Hunch got the key and Elwood got his big flashlight.

As Scott started down the basement steps there was an odd tingling sensation along his spine. He had a premonition of discovery. The feeling that they were at last coming close to the truth—to that elusive clue which had been evading him and Elwood.

13

Blue Eyes and Footprints

THEY ALL HAD a share in checking the contents of the old trunk in the cellar. This time, however, the search was more thorough. The photographs were examined, one by one; the piles of letters and clippings were divided and carefully read.

Even Bluebell had a part in the search, getting in everyone's way and sticking her curious little face down into the trunk to see the relics.

"Why didn't you leave that nuisance upstairs, Elwood?" demanded Mr. Carter in disgust as Bluebell almost poked him in the eye with a small ivory fan.

"Didn't think of it," said Elwood. He laid aside a pile of letters. "Guess there's nothing here we didn't see before," he remarked.

Then, as they were about to give up, it was Bluebell who found what they were looking for. She dug down behind the torn lining of the trunk and came up with a wadded scrap of paper. Saucily she threw it right in Mr. Carter's face.

He picked it up, started to toss it aside, then thoughtfully straightened it out. "Why, it's a telegram," he said in surprise. "To Mrs. Truelove from her son. It announces the birth of Claretta Ann Truelove. . . . It's sent from San Diego, California. And listen to this." Mr. Carter's voice rose with excitement. " 'If you want to send flowers, Mother, they are at Mercy Hospital.' "

"That proves she was born in San Diego," said Mr. Hunch. "That's what the lawyer wanted to know."

"But why?" queried Scott.

It was Patty who answered that. She had been taking a last look at the baby book Mrs. Truelove had kept for her son. That was her cue. "For footprints, of course," she cried. "Don't you remember, Scott—in our baby books at home Mother has little cards she got at the hospital with our footprints on them?"

"That's right," said Scott. "The hospital made them of all the new babies so they wouldn't get the babies mixed up. Do you suppose they'll still have those prints on file in San Diego, Dad?" he asked his father.

"Of course they would," Elwood said. "It's routine." He spoke with authority, as though he'd had this idea in mind all along. "All we have to do is get Linda's footprints and send them to the hospital, and they'll compare them with—"

"What are we waiting for, then?" cried Patty, jumping up. "Let's go get Linda's footprints right away."

Then she stopped and added lamely, "Oh, I guess we'll have to get the police or somebody to do it. We haven't any footprint ink."

"That's what you think," Elwood said. "I can mix some up in my lab in a jiffy. Come on, Bluebell, let's go see Linda."

"It's pretty late, Elwood," Mr. Hunch protested. "The girl will be in bed by now."

"Oh, please," Patty was pleading. "Linda will be just as anxious as we are to find out."

"Well, make it snappy, kids." Mr. Carter made the decision. Then he got up and helped Mr. Hunch push the trunk back while the children went upstairs to perform their odd errand.

Patty held Bluebell while Elwood got the ink. Then they went up to the third floor and knocked at number six.

Linda came to the door, blinking her eyes sleepily. "What's the matter?" she asked. A dim bedside lamp was the only light in the room.

Patty explained what they wanted, and, slightly dazed by it all, Linda obediently sat in a chair while Elwood painted the bottom of her feet with his ink. Then Patty pressed each foot firmly on a piece of white paper.

Meanwhile Bluebell got loose and jumped on the bed. She managed to turn a somersault and tipped the lamp shade down before Scott could catch her.

"We'll write a letter first thing in the morning,

Linda," Elwood said, getting to his feet. "This will settle the whole business once and for all."

"If they have the footprints of the Truelove baby on file in that hospital," Scott said, "and they match yours, you'll own this house, and you can kick Bluebell out."

He said it teasingly, but Linda didn't know. "Oh, I would never do that, Scott," she said warmly. "If I am the heiress and get this house, Bluebell will have her little apartment as long as she lives. And you, too, Elwood," she added, "you and your father can always live here. That was my grandmother's—I mean, Mrs. Truelove's—wish. And it is mine."

Patty brought a wet towel from the bathroom for Linda to wipe the ink off her feet. Then she gave Linda a quick impulsive little hug and left with the boys.

Before he bid them good night and went with Blue-bell up into the attic, Elwood said a surprising thing. "I hope now that Linda *is* the right one. But I've still got that funny feeling. It's like putting a puzzle together and finding you've got one piece out of the wrong box."

Regretfully, Scott realized that he felt the same way. And if the right piece to the puzzle was in that trunk in the cellar, they had missed it again. "Well, we'll send those footprints in the morning," he said. "And then we'll know."

It was Mr. Hunch who finally pointed out the false piece in the puzzle, and then it was quite by accident.

Linda went off to work without any of them seeing her the next morning. The three young people were in Elwood's apartment working in the little corner Mr. Hunch used as his office.

They had just typed out their letter to the hospital in San Diego, and had put it in a big envelope with Linda's footprints, when Mr. Hunch came in.

He picked up the letter with a smile. "I sure hope Linda gets this place instead of those cousins," he remarked. "If she really is Mrs. Truelove's granddaughter, she came to this house fifteen years ago. And she was the sweetest little blue-eyed angel you ever saw in your—"

"What did you say?" Scott Carter sprang from his chair.

Mr. Hunch started to repeat his words, then stopped. A puzzled frown spread slowly over his long face. At the same time Elwood shouted, "That's it! That's what's wrong, Scott. Linda Blake can't possibly be Claretta Truelove. That little girl had blue eyes, and Linda's are *brown."*

"Why, of course." Patty's eyes were bleak. "In that letter in the trunk from Mrs. Truelove's son he spoke of the little blue-eyed baby. But it could have been a mistake," she said hopefully. "Sometimes babies' eyes turn brown later on."

"Not this baby's eyes," Elwood insisted. "The father had blue eyes; it said so in that baby book. And the mother was Swedish, wasn't she, Pa?" He turned to Mr. Hunch.

His father nodded. "Yes, I remember her. She was a tall, good-looking blond woman with blue eyes."

"Two blue-eyed parents can never have a brown-eyed child," Elwood said. "I've read about it. It is genetically impossible, according to Mendel's theory of heredity. Blue eyes are recessive in the genes."

That seemed to be that. Scott didn't doubt the truth of the statement, and he felt suddenly tired.

"There's no use sending the letter then, is there?" he said.

Patty was near to tears. "I think we should go down

and see Linda," she said. "I know she'll be disappointed, but I want her to know I still trust her."

"Well, I don't know what to think." Elwood looked very confused. "If she isn't Claretta Truelove—which she isn't—and if she isn't in cahoots with Caleb Jones, which she may be, how did she know about this old house?"

"Maybe she has extrasensory perception," said Scott jokingly.

But nobody laughed.

14

The False Clue

THEY HAD just stepped through the front door when Patty suddenly became aware of the fact that Bluebell was with them—perched on Elwood's shoulder. She stopped on the step, and to Scott's surprise, stamped her foot.

"Elwood Hunch," she cried. "You are not going to bring that pesky animal along to the sweet shop."

Scott and Elwood stared at her, shocked at this behavior. It was the first time Patty had ever taken out her anger on Bluebell.

"You remember what happened the last time," she went on. "Bluebell ruined that man's sundae and ate his cherry. We just have too much to worry about today to bother with her. You take her back into the house," she demanded.

Elwood looked crestfallen. And Bluebell actually hissed at Patty.

"I can't leave her with Pa," Elwood said. "He has to go to town on busines."

"Then Mother can watch her." Patty took Bluebell's leash, but Scott shook his head at that.

"Mother has an appointment with the dentist," he reminded her.

Just then the window on the second floor above them opened. Mrs. Penny stuck her head out. "What's the trouble down there?" she asked sweetly.

"We have to go someplace," Patty explained. She didn't say where. "Elwood wants to take Bluebell along, and we just *can't*, that's all."

"Why, I'll be glad to watch Bluebell for you, Elwood. Just wait right there."

"Well?" said Patty, glaring defiantly at Elwood while Mrs. Penny was coming down. "You said yourself you could trust her, and she baby-sat with Bluebell before, didn't she?"

Elwood scratched his head nervously. "I guess it's all right this time," he said. "We won't be gone long."

He handed Bluebell's leash to Mrs. Penny, who had just come through the door.

"I'll take good care of her," she said brightly. She had brought some peanuts and was trying to put them into the pocket of the red jacket which she had made for the monkey, but the pocket was already full of trinkets Bluebell had picked up.

Mrs. Penny laughed. "Here, Elwood, you take care

of her treasures." She gave him a handful of odds and ends which Elwood stuck in his own pocket: a bottle top, a few rocks, something that looked like a pill box.

"We'll just go for a walk out in the backyard," she promised. "She'll be fine."

Elwood looked a little dazed by now. "Don't let her eat any green crab apples, Mrs. Penny," he begged.

As they moved away Scott saw the monkey give Mrs. Penny a big smack on the cheek. She laughed heartily. She *was* a kind woman, thought Scott.

It was almost noon when they reached the sweet shop. Linda was very busy and looked flustered.

Someone was yelling for a cup of coffee when Patty and the boys walked in. Another customer—the same fat man they had seen there before—was complaining loudly that Linda had given him chocolate chip when he ordered cherry vanilla.

Scott, Patty, and Elwood slipped onto the only three remaining stools in the place.

"Maybe we'd better go away and come back later," Scott whispered to Patty. "We certainly can't tell her about it now, when she's so busy." He hated to break the bad news.

"Let's just wait a little while and get a Coke," said Patty.

Just then Linda herself came up and faced them. She reached out and wiped the counter in front of Scott. There was a strange look on her face.

"What will you have, sir?" Her starched hat was

twisted on her golden head and she looked toward him
with a blank stare.

"*Sir?*" Scott repeated the word. "Linda, what's the
matter? I'm Scott, don't you know me—?" He suddenly
stuttered. Then shouted crazily.

"*She has blue eyes!*"

Patty was staring, too. And Elwood. "She has, she
has," whispered Patty. "Beautiful big blue eyes!"

"Of course I have," Linda said somewhat crossly.
"And they may be beautiful, but they're also near-
sighted. I've misplaced my contact lenses," she added,
suddenly tearful, "And I can hardly see."

Someone at the other end of the counter was rapping with his spoon. "Where's my coffee? I'm in a hurry, miss!"

Two tears were rolling down Linda's pretty face and she wiped them away with the back of her hand. She got the cup of coffee, and she spilled it as she set it down.

"That's enough," said the manager, who had been watching from the rear. He came up behind the counter. "You can leave now, Miss Blake," he told Linda. "You've been making mistakes all morning—giving lemon for vanilla, and chocolate for raspberry—"

He was shaking his head. "Just go," he pleaded when Linda hesitated.

By now Patty, Scott, and Elwood were standing up. Their faces were jubilant. "Come on, Linda," urged Patty. "You aren't going to need this old job anyway. You're going to inherit a fortune!"

"What happened to your contact lenses?" Scott asked when they were outside. He put his hand on Linda's elbow to pilot her down the street.

"I don't know." She was laughing now, so relieved to be out of the hectic sweet shop. "I put them on the table beside my bed last night, and this morning I just couldn't find them. They must have fallen."

"Did you have them on last night when we came to get those footprints?" asked Scott.

"The room wasn't very light," said Elwood, "or we

would have seen your blue eyes then. I wonder what became of—" He stopped short. "Wait a minute!"

He reached into his pocket and drew out the trinkets Mrs. Penny had taken from Bluebell's pocket. "Is this yours?" he asked, holding out the little box.

Linda took the tiny plastic box and looked at it closely. "Yes," she said happily. "Where did you find it?"

"In somebody's pocket," Scott said with a sigh. They didn't need to explain further, and Linda laughed with delight.

As soon as they reached the Tower Arms she sat on the porch step. She opened the little box and showed the three what was inside—two tiny brown plastic disks, not much larger than fishscales. With the help of a small mirror from her purse, she popped the disks, one at a time, over the irises of her eyes.

She blinked twice, and magically her eyes were brown once more.

"But why do you wear brown ones," demanded Patty, "when you have such lovely blue eyes?"

Linda smiled. "Oh, I have blue ones, too; and green ones. Mother and Father spoiled me, and when I was sixteen they got me contacts in three colors to go with my different dresses. When I came to Nebraska, I packed in such a hurry, I just brought the ones I was wearing. I'm so used to them I didn't even think of telling you my eyes were *blue*."

"Well, if it hadn't been for Bluebell," Patty began, "we would still be—"

"*Bluebell.*" Elwood had been sitting beside Linda, beaming with admiration. At the mention of the monkey's name he was on his feet. "I'd better check up on her," he said. "Let's try Mrs. Penny's apartment."

Scott and Elwood bounded up the stairs and rapped on the door of number four. The moment the plump little woman opened her door, they knew something was wrong.

"Where's Bluebell?" Elwood asked.

Mrs. Penny's face was red and wet with tears. She was twisting a handkerchief in her hand. "Oh, Elwood," she said, "something dreadful has happened. Bluebell is gone. She broke away from me and disappeared through the trees. I called her and called her, and looked around everywhere. I've just now come up to call the police."

Then she turned her head suddenly and spoke over her shoulder. "I'm coming, dear," she said shakily. "Mr. Penny needs me—"

But the boys were already on their way down the stairs. When Linda and Patty heard the bad news, they joined in the search for the lost pet. At first they all ran here and there in the neighborhood, making a haphazard search of roofs and treetops.

Then they calmed down a little and met in front of the big house. "We've got to be methodical about this,"

said Elwood. "First, let's ask everyone in the building if they've seen any sign of her."

He was trying—they were all trying—to believe that this was just a mischievous prank of Bluebell's and that she would turn up any minute. They were soon to learn that the situation was much more serious.

Scott knocked on Caleb Jones's door, and there was no answer. He knocked again, louder. Then he pushed the door open.

Caleb was gone and his room was in great disorder. It looked as though the artist had gone in a hurry.

It was Miss Twittengale who provided the only likely clue as to what may have happened to Bluebell—when they rapped at her door.

"No," she said, "I haven't seen Miss Bluebell. I seldom go out, you know, because of my hay fever. I take my exercise in the halls—"

"Well, have you seen anything unusual at all today?" Scott asked anxiously over Elwood's shoulder.

The little gray-haired woman frowned. "I did see something odd about an hour ago," she admitted. "I was looking out of my side window, and I saw a taxi drive up to the corner on the next street. A man got into it, and he had a big box—like a crate."

"Was the man Caleb Jones?"

"Well, I don't know, but he was wearing a brown jacket."

Just then Mr. Hunch returned from his trip to town. When the anxious quartet filled him in on the alarming situation, he suggested calling the cab company. "Maybe they can tell us where the fellow went."

Mr. Hunch went to the telephone and called a friend he knew. Scott and his companions stood waiting while the man at the other end of the line checked with the cab drivers.

Elwood's father turned from the phone looking unusually grim. "Something fishy here, all right. One of the drivers picked up some fellow in the next block and took him to the airport. Said he had a crate with an animal in it. The driver didn't know what kind of animal—but it was awful noisy."

15

One-way Ticket for Bluebell

"COME ON!" said Mr. Hunch.

His car was parked at the curb. They all piled in, and in another moment they were on their way to the airport.

The Lincoln Airport was a busy place. One huge plane was coming in and others were preparing to take off. Summer travelers moved busily about the terminal.

Scott and his four companions burst through the door and paused to look anxiously around. Where was Bluebell? Was she even now on her way to some unknown city?

There was no time to waste.

"Let's split up," cried Scott, taking charge. "Elwood, you go to the baggage office—find out if anyone has checked a monkey today. Patty and Linda—look around behind the terminal. If you see Caleb Jones getting on a plane yell your heads off!"

"I'll check the ticket offices," said Mr. Hunch grimly.

They flew in all directions.

Scott himself moved toward a row of benches, in front of a huge window that overlooked the airfield, scanning every face as he went. A number of people waited on the benches—two salesmen with bulging sample cases, a pilot chatting with a friend, a little old woman. There was no sign of Caleb.

Scott started to turn away when something caught his eye. Lying on one of the benches was a man's brown sport coat. He moved closer, not taking his eye from the coat for a second. It had a row of round leather buttons with a spiral design. *The bottom button was missing.*

Leaving the coat just as he found it, Scott tore through the building in search of Elwood. Elwood was just coming from the baggage room on his way to the door. Scott grabbed his arm.

"Give me that button," he demanded.

The other boy turned, his long face blank. "What button?"

"The one you said Bluebell grabbed off somebody's coat in the attic."

"Oh, that." Elwood reached in his pocket and pulled out a leather button. He dropped it into Scott's outstretched hand. "What's up? Did you find Caleb Jones?"

"No, but I think I've found that coat! Come with me."

They ran back toward the row of benches, but when

Scott reached the spot where he had seen the coat, he stopped in dismay. It was gone.

Just then Mr. Hunch arrived. He too was shaking his head. "No luck at the ticket offices. If anybody from Tower Arms took a plane today, he used a false name. One man told me to try the baggage office if we're looking for animals."

"No luck there either," said Elwood. "Baggage man said he did check something in with a special permit —thought it was a dog, though."

Scott looked past the benches to the airfield. "That man with the brown coat could be getting on a plane this very minute," he said, frowning.

Almost in answer to his worried remark, a voice droned over the loud speaker. "Flight seventy-six now loading. Omaha . . . Kansas City . . . Chicago."

"Let's go," said Elwood.

They rushed outdoors, to the side of the building, where they found Patty and Linda still frantically looking for Bluebell.

"I know she's here somewhere," said the excited Patty when she saw her brother. "We heard some men talking about a 'blasted monkey,' didn't we, Linda?"

"Yes." Linda's face was flushed. "They said she tried to bite—"

At that instant a weird noise was heard. A shrill whistle, followed by a familiar and angry screech.

"*Bluebell!*" cried Linda.

The noise grew louder. It was coming from a crate

on a small luggage cart that was passing by. And that cart was being wheeled toward the big plane that was preparing to take off!

Patty Carter went into action. Like a small golden whirlwind, she flew toward an untended gate in the fence that cut off the field. She was through it in seconds and running after the luggage cart. Linda was right behind her.

"Bluebell," Patty screamed. "Don't worry, we'll save you."

She reached the cart just as it was being moved under the belly of the big plane.

The man handling the cart turned and saw Patty. "Go back, young lady," he said curtly. "Passengers aren't allowed on this part of the field."

"I'm not a passenger," Patty answered impatiently. "You've got our monkey there and we want her."

By now the others had arrived. Mr. Hunch spoke up.

"That's right," he said to the man. "There's been some mistake. The animal in that crate has been stolen. She's the famous monkey that inherited the Truelove estate. You can't put her on that plane."

A big door in the plane was opening above them. The man began to hand suitcases to someone up above.

"I've got my orders, mister," he said to Elwood's father. He puffed as he bent down to look at the tag on Bluebell's crate. "This monkey is consigned to the Borneo Sewing Machine Company in New York, and that's where it's going to go."

He put his hands on the crate. But to his surprise it slipped right out of his grasp. Elwood and Scott had taken over. They pulled the cage, monkey and all, to the ground.

Bluebell looked out through the bars and showed her teeth at the irate man. And Patty, desperate now, jumped on top of the crate and stayed there.

"If you take Bluebell to New York," she said stubbornly, "you'll have to take me too."

By now two more field attendants had come on the scene. They pushed Elwood and Scott aside and confronted Patty. "Get off of there, girlie," said the biggest one. "We've got to load this crate."

Patty didn't budge.

Meanwhile someone had called the manager of the air freight office. He arrived just about then, fuming and snorting.

"What's the trouble here?" he demanded. "Flight 76 is already late. Get that stuff loaded and put this plane in the air."

Then he looked around at the five determined representatives from the Tower Arms. "Until this animal reaches its proper destination," he stated, "it is the responsibility of the airline. You people get off this field, or I shall have to call the police."

"Don't bother," said Mr. Hunch. "I was just about to call them myself. This monkey is stolen property, and I don't intend to let her leave the ground." He turned to go, then added over his shoulder: "Elwood, don't you give an inch. Stay right here and guard that monkey with your life."

The manager of the air freight office stalked after him.

When the three field attendants had loaded the rest of the luggage they moved to one side to await developments. Patty continued to sit on the cage. And Linda bent down to talk to the nervous Bluebell in her gentle, soothing voice.

While all this was going on, Scott Carter had been quietly studying Bluebell's prison. It was made of wood and was large enough for the little animal to move about in. In fact, it was surprisingly large.

The door was secured with a small padlock. The key was taped to the outside.

At first Scott thought of unlocking the crate and letting Bluebell escape. But he realized that she might scamper away and never be caught.

Then all at once a wild inspiration came to him. While the men were talking among themselves he reached down, tore the key loose, and unlocked the padlock. Linda moved aside.

At the same time he whispered to his sister, "Get down, Pat, and when I open this door, jump inside."

Patty needed only the suggestion. She slipped from the crate; Scott yanked open the door. In a flash Patty was inside with Bluebell, crouched down on her knees.

The men were now alerted by the sound of the door, but before they could interfere, Scott slammed it shut and snapped the lock. When he held the key in front of the cage Bluebell snatched it and put it in her pocket.

So Flight 76 was forced to leave without Bluebell. Even the workmen had to laugh as they moved the cage to a safe spot so the plane could take off.

"That's just where you belong, young lady," said one of them to Patty, "in a monkey cage."

Patty wasn't too comfortable in there but she grinned back.

"Don't be too uppity," said the man with a laugh. "You've saved your monkey for the moment. But she'll be on the next flight."

Then things began to happen again. It suddenly became apparent that both Mr. Hunch and the airport official had gotten through to the police, for two police cars drove up from opposite directions. Four uniformed men got out and stood staring at the monkey cage in disbelief.

It was obvious that they could not allow the airline to send Patty to New York with the cargo, so one of the men politely asked for the key to unlock the cage.

Patty smiled sweetly through the bars. "Ask Bluebell," she said. "She has the key now."

But Bluebell showed only her teeth. So the sergeant sent to his car for a file and had the lock filed off. When he opened the door at last, Patty crawled out meekly, and Bluebell came after her and perched on her shoulder.

The officer looked helplessly at the defiant group in front of him—Scott, Patty, Elwood, Linda, Mr. Hunch, and the glaring Bluebell. Finally he went back to the police car and radioed the station to talk to the chief himself.

When he returned, he told Mr. Hunch that to prevent Bluebell from being shipped off on the next flight, he would have to get an injunction.

"That means," he said, "you'll have to get an order from the court to hold her here. Then we'll take her down to the station and impound her until this matter is settled."

Mr. Hunch hastened off to see his lawyer to get the proper paper. The police officer instructed Patty to put Bluebell back in her cage. Then it was wired up so the little creature could not escape.

"You take good care of her," Patty said, sniffing a little. Linda came up and put her arm around Patty's shoulders.

At last the paddy wagon drove up and Bluebell was hauled away, scolding and hissing, to spend some time in jail. Patty, Scott, Linda, and Elwood looked wistfully after the disappearing vehicle.

16

Miss Claretta Truelove

"WELL, AT LEAST we kept Bluebell from being carted off to New York," said Scott gratefully as Mr. Hunch drove them all back to the apartment house.

"Yes, siree!" said Mr. Hunch. "That sure was quick thinking, Scott. If it hadn't been for you and Patty, we might never have seen Bluebell again. Elwood must have been right all along when he suspected that one of those seven cousins was up to mischief."

"I'd like to get my hands on that monkeynabber," said Elwood. "I'm sure now it was Caleb Jones. He's probably on his way to New York on that plane."

Scott looked up into the blue Nebraska sky and grinned. "If he is," he said, "he's going to be awfully disappointed when he gets there. He'll find some of his baggage left behind!"

"I still find it hard to believe it was Caleb," said Linda thoughtfully. "Only this morning he was in the sweet shop. He asked me to go to a concert at Pershing Center and he was worrying because he couldn't find his best shirt."

"He was just trying to butter you up, Linda," said Patty grimly. "He's the guilty one, all right. He— Why, there he is now!" she cried then.

Mr. Hunch had just driven up in front of the Tower Arms, and at that very moment Caleb Jones was coming out of the door. He was loaded down with what appeared to be a great bundle of laundry wrapped in a sheet.

The five occupants of the car stared at him, dumfounded.

"Why he didn't take the plane to New York after all," muttered Elwood. "He must have checked Bluebell through and then rushed right back here so he wouldn't be suspected."

Caleb Jones put down his bundle and approached the car. He wasn't wearing the brown jacket now, if indeed he had ever worn it. His lean face bore a look of concern as he peered into the car.

"Didn't you find Bluebell?" he asked. "Mrs. Penny told me she had escaped. I'm really sorry, Elwood. She was a noisy little rascal, I'll admit, but the old house won't seem the same without her."

Linda, seated beside Scott, was about to reassure Caleb as to Bluebell's welfare, but Scott squeezed her arm warningly.

"You don't see her, do you, Mr. Jones?" he asked

coldly as he stepped out of the car. He wasn't about to be fooled by the artist's show of concern.

"It's too bad," Caleb went on, oblivious to the unfriendly response. "I'm sorry I wasn't around to help in the search. I've been cleaning out closets, taking things to the cleaners—"

Patty was so angry she didn't even look at Caleb as she got out of the car. When Linda stopped to chat with him, Patty grabbed her and pushed her right up the steps and into the house.

"Don't even speak to him!" she scolded.

Miss Twittengale was waiting for them in the lower hall. She too expressed her sympathy to Elwood. Scott thought he saw a jubilant gleam in her eyes. Why should this mild little music teacher look so happy? he wondered. Was it because she alone had been involved in the plot to kidnap Bluebell?

By now he fully expected Mrs. Penny to pop out at the second floor and shed a few more tears over her carelessness in letting the monkey get away. But Mrs. Penny was letting the television man into her apartment and didn't seem to notice the group's return.

Elwood and his father stayed downstairs, and Linda left Scott and Patty at the door of number six. She was tired after the strain of the past few hours and said she was going to rest.

Scott realized that he was tired too, and when he and his sister finally landed in their own apartment, all they could do was collapse onto the couch.

"I'm beat," remarked Scott.

"So am I," said Patty. She blinked her eyes a little. "I can't keep from thinking about poor Bluebell, all by herself in that old jail."

Just then Mrs. Carter came in from the kitchen. She looked concerned. "I don't wonder you're beat, as you call it," she declared. "You haven't had any lunch. And what's this about Bluebell being in jail? Mrs. Penny told me she got away. . . . Now, for goodness sake, come into the kitchen and tell me what happened while I fix you something to eat."

Patty and Scott sat at the kitchen table while their mother warmed soup and made sandwiches. As they ate they told her about the wild events at the airport and how Patty had saved Bluebell by getting herself locked in the cage.

Mrs. Carter laughed till the tears ran down her cheeks. But she grew sober a moment later when she remembered how serious the matter was.

"Elwood's fears were well founded, after all," she said. "It's hard to believe that there is anybody under this roof who would commit a crime just to get Mrs. Truelove's money a little sooner."

"Well, whoever tried to shanghai Bluebell is going to get a shock when they find out she hasn't gone to New York at all," Scott said with satisfaction.

"They'll be even more shocked," Patty added, "when they discover that Mrs. Truelove's lost granddaughter is right here at Tower Arms and they may never inherit a penny of—"

"Wait, Pat!" Scott put his glass of milk down with a little bang. "We never sent that letter—the one with Linda's footprints! We got so upset over her having brown eyes—"

Patty jumped to her feet. "It's probably lying on Mr. Hunch's desk this very minute."

Mrs. Carter laughed. "Oh, no it isn't," she said. "It's in the wastebasket at your father's office—the envelope, that is. When I went down to the dentist this morning I stopped at Mr. Hunch's apartment for a minute. He was just going out, and he handed me your letter to mail. He said there was some doubt now about Linda's being the heiress, but he thought the letter should be sent anyway. He didn't explain."

"But how did Dad get the letter?" Scott asked impatiently.

"I took it to his office, but he said we shouldn't mail it. He is just as anxious to help prove Linda's claim as you are, so he took the footprints to a man in the district attorney's office. They have a code for relaying prints, and he asked them to wire San Diego, describing Linda's prints. If they match those of the Truelove baby born there, the San Diego authorities are to wire back."

Patty and Scott were still mulling over this latest bit of news when someone knocked at the door. It was

Elwood. He too had remembered the footprint matter and was coming to tell them that the letter was gone from his father's desk.

As Scott was explaining the situation to him, the phone in the kitchen rang. Mrs. Carter came out a moment later, beaming.

"That was your father, Scott. He just heard from San Diego. A little girl was born at Mercy Hospital there almost twenty-one years ago. Her name was Claretta Ann Truelove, and her footprints exactly match those of Linda Blake."

"Hooray!" Scott made a standing jump, touching the

ceiling with his fingertips. "Linda is the real heiress!"

"Let's go tell her," cried Patty, running for the door. Elwood, just as pleased as the Carters now, joined them in taking the good news to Linda. She returned with them a moment later, looking dazed and excited.

Mrs. Carter looked at her and cried out: "You have blue eyes!"

"Of course she has," said Patty. "She has been asleep and isn't wearing her contact lenses." She explained to her mother the confusion over the color of Linda's eyes and how it had convinced them that she could not be the heiress.

"We'll have to have a big celebration for you, Linda," Mrs. Carter said happily. "I'll bake a cake."

Scott had a better idea. "Let's have another party for everyone in the house tomorrow night," he suggested.

"We'll announce Linda's good news and whoever kidnaped Bluebell will be so surprised he'll give himself away."

"Will the seven cousins ever get a shock!" put in Patty gleefully.

"I hope it works," added Elwood. His long face still showed his worry over his beloved pet. "The judge told Pa that if whoever it was left Bluebell at the airport would sign a release, we could get her back without any trouble. Otherwise there will be a lot of red tape."

Thinking of the caged Bluebell, they all grew serious. "We can't make whoever it is sign unless we know who it is," said Patty.

It was then that Linda spoke for the first time. A change had come over her. Knowing who she was, at long last, had given her confidence.

"We'll get the truth," she said grimly, "if we have to *drag* it out of them."

17

All Buttoned Up

THE SURPRISE announcement party for Linda was held in the garden behind the Truelove mansion. It was a lovely summer evening and everybody came—even Mr. Penny, who was rarely seen by the other tenants except when they visited the Pennys' apartment. Mr. Carter had insisted.

"Poor old fellow," he had said when Mrs. Penny mentioned that it was difficult for her husband to get up and down the steps. "He's up there by himself so much, with nothing to do but stare at that television. He's coming to this party if Hunch and I have to carry him down bodily."

That's just about what they did. Mr. Hunch and Scott's father trundled the wheelchair down the long flight of stairs—with Mr. Penny, gray and rigid, sitting in it. They wheeled him into the backyard and under a big elm tree near the table.

Everyone was kind and helpful. Caleb Jones sat on

the grass near him and chatted about the weather. Miss Twittengale watched his plate and saw that he had plenty of ice cream and cake.

Linda looked beautiful in a filmy yellow dress, and Scott and Patty wore their dress-up clothes and waited on everybody. The only important person missing was Bluebell, thought Scott, and how she would have loved it all!

Elwood himself, who had been completely won over by Linda, had been chosen to make the exciting announcement. But before he rose to speak, Miss Twittengale had something to say.

She stood up while the cake was being served. "I just can't keep my good news any longer," she declared. "As some of you know, I've been expecting to come into a little money. Well, it came today—my very first social security check, and I made a down payment on a brand-new piano! You'll be hearing much sweeter music from number two," she added, and ended with an unexpected sneeze.

She sat down amid loud clapping. Scott grinned. "That let's her off the hook," he whispered to Patty. "She takes walks in the halls because of her hay fever, and her fortune comes from the government. That makes Caleb look more guilty than ever."

Then Elwood got up and cleared his throat. He had a little speech all ready to give, but at the last minute he forgot it. He just looked at Linda and said: "Miss Twittengale's news was pretty good, all right, but

Linda's got some news that's even better yet. We just found out by taking her footprints. She's the real heiress to this property. She's Claretta Truelove, the lost granddaughter of old Mrs.—"

"What's that?" The hoarse shout came from the direction of the elm tree. And suddenly Mr. Penny, who had never been seen to move his legs, rose halfway out of his wheelchair. His face was like a thunder cloud. "What did you say?"

Elwood stammered, "She—she—"

"Wait, Elwood!" In that split second Scott had seen something. In one bound he was out of his chair and

across the lawn. He pulled the blanket from Mr. Penny's knees. When the man rose from his chair, Scott had noticed the buttons on his brown jacket. And, as he suspected, the bottom button was missing!

Scott took the leather button Elwood had given him from among the odds and ends he always carried in his pocket. It exactly matched those on the jacket.

By now Mr. Penny was spluttering in a self-conscious manner. "Where—where'd you get that, boy?" he demanded.

"Oh, dear," said Mrs. Penny from somewhere behind Scott. She sat down in her chair with a little plop.

"I got it from Elwood, Mr. Penny," Scott answered sharply. He turned to the other boy. "You tell him where he lost it, Elwood."

Elwood had caught on by now. His face was dark and accusing as he pointed at the man in the wheelchair. "You're the one who broke into Bluebell's attic a few weeks ago and tried to kidnap her. She tore that button off your jacket."

"And you must be the one who *did* kidnap Bluebell today," said Scott. "You went to the airport and—"

The man in the chair was white-faced and spluttering. "A lot of nonsense," he retorted. "How could I do a thing like that? I'm a cripple. Can't walk a step—"

There was a little moan then from Mrs. Penny. She got up and came to stand beside her husband. "It's no use, Carl," she said. "They know now that we are the guilty ones. Besides, the Truelove fortune is lost anyway. The will made it very clear that if Mrs. Truelove's immediate heirs turned up, you would get nothing."

"Then you *are* one of the cousins?" Scott said.

"Yes." The plump woman nodded, her face pink with shame. "That is, *he* is," she added, pointing to her husband. "He is really Abigail Truelove's second cousin. I met him a few years ago when he came to California. There are six other heirs, too, you know," she added. "They all got together and decided that Abigail's will was terribly unfair—"

"Ridiculous business!" muttered Mr. Penny from his chair. "Leaving all that fortune to a *monkey*."

"So you all cooked up a plot to get Bluebell out of the picture so the cousins would get possession of the estate right away?" This was from Mr. Carter. He and everyone in the party were now standing around the Pennys, listening in amazement to the disgraceful confession.

"And Penny is no more crippled than I am," said Mr. Hunch, looking very disillusioned.

"No." Mrs. Penny smiled wanly and patted her husband on the shoulder. "He just pretended to be, and whenever anyone came to our apartment, he got in the wheelchair in front of the television."

"But I still don't understand how he kidnaped Bluebell." Scott was frowning. "He never went out of the house, and today when Elwood and I knocked on your door, he was there—"

She shook her gray head. "No, he had already taken

Bluebell to the airport. I just pretended he was calling to me. He came and went quite often, and had that cage made at the lumberyard and kept it ready, hidden under some bushes in the next block. Of course he was disguised. He wore working clothes and a black wig and glasses."

The truth dawned suddenly on Scott. "The television man!" he cried.

"We saw him come and go all the time," sighed Linda, "and never suspected."

"That's the way it was," Mrs. Penny admitted sadly. Then she made one final admission. "And our name isn't really Penny. My husband belongs to the Boston branch of the family. He is Carl Jackson."

"Carl Jackson!" It was Patty who echoed the name. She turned and pointed to Caleb Jones, who was standing beside her. "Why, we thought *you* were Carl Jackson, Mr. Jones."

"Me?" Caleb had been holding a huge hunk of cake in his hand, too surprised by the turn of events to eat it. "Why me?"

"Because your initials are the same—Caleb Jones; Carl Jackson. And because you always acted so—so suspicious." Patty flushed a little.

Caleb laughed. "Well, it's just a coincidence about my name," he declared. "Besides, my real name is Phineas Caleb Jones. And as for acting suspicious, I guess I am a little temperamental at times."

Nobody answered that, and it was about then that

Mr. Penny—or Mr. Jackson, that is—decided to give
up his absurd pretense of being unable to walk. He got
out of the wheelchair and gave it a push backward.

"What do we do now?" he asked defiantly. "I suppose you intend to call the authorities and have us
arrested for sending that useless monkey off to New
York. If my wife hadn't wanted to come to this party
we'd already be out of town," he added.

Linda finally spoke up. In spite of her threatened
firmness, her voice was gentle and wondering. "Why
were you sending Bluebell to New York?" she asked.

The false Mrs. Penny's eyes filled with tears. "We
didn't want to hurt the dear little thing," she said. "One
of the cousins—Winston Truelove—is a salesman for the
Borneo Sewing Machine Company. He was going to
take her to Borneo and turn her loose with the wild
monkeys. . . . Oh, it was a terrible thing to do!"

"I think it can all be forgotten," Linda said, "if we
can just get Bluebell back home and—"

At that very moment, as though in answer to her
name, there was a familiar sound of raucous chattering, and two uniformed men came around the corner
of the Truelove mansion, carrying the monkey cage
between them. Through the slats Scott saw the bright
brown eyes of the furious little prisoner.

The two policemen put the cage in front of Elwood.

"There's your wretched beast," said one of them,
mopping his forehead with a handkerchief. "We've
had all we can stand of her down at the station, and

the chief got permission from the judge to put her back in your custody till the case is settled."

"She's been raising a terrible rumpus," the other officer said. "The chief can't concentrate, and the prisoners can get no rest at all."

Before the men had finished speaking, Elwood had unwired the cage, with Patty hovering impatiently behind him.

"Bluebell!" the girl cried as the little animal crept, blinking and bedraggled, out of the cage. Patty seized her lovingly. Everyone present, even Mr. and Mrs. Carl Jackson, looked grateful at this fortunate turn of events.

Miss Bluebell, realizing that she was free and safely home, came to life in a hurry. She shook hands all around, pulled the jubilant Elwood's long nose, and then—in an ecstasy of good will—she leaned over and bestowed a big wet kiss on the cheek of the person next to her.

That happened to be Caleb Jones.

Caleb looked stunned for a moment. Then he began to beam. "Why, I believe she likes me," he said.

"Of course she does," said Miss Claretta Truelove, formerly known as Linda. "Bluebell is a smart little monkey." And she looked up at Caleb with her big, admiring brown eyes, which were really blue, of course.

Scott Carter, standing to one side, looked at Patty Carter and smiled. He could almost hear the satisfied sigh of the big old Truelove mansion as it settled back

on its foundations. . . . Linda and Bluebell—the two lost heiresses—were back where they belonged.

He took a small leather object from his pocket and stared at it. The mystery was solved, the case all buttoned up. With a grin, Scott tossed the button to the man in the brown jacket.

Sadly, Carl Jackson caught it.